Raif searched her expression for dishonesty... Instead he found himself drinking in her beauty.

"Ann..." he breathed.

When she spoke, the anger had unexpectedly left her tone, replaced by what sounded like wariness. "What do you want me to say, Raif?"

It wasn't what he wanted her to say. It was what he wanted her to do. And that had nothing to do with his family's statue.

"How can I end this?" she asked.

He pulled his thoughts back from the brink. "Give me my statue."

"That's impossible."

Raif took a step closer, crowding her, determined to get this farce over with. "In Rayas we would not ask so politely."

"We're not in Rayas."

"Pity."

"Why? If we were in Ray~~as~~ me in a dungeon?"

"If we were in Ray~~as~~

A GOLDEN BETRAYAL

BY
BARBARA DUNLOP

MILLS
BOON

First published in Great Britain 2013
by Mills & Boon, an imprint of Harlequin (UK) Limited,
Harlequin (UK) Limited, Eton House, 18-24 Paradise Road,
Richmond, Surrey TW9 1SR

© Harlequin S.A 2012

Special thanks and acknowledgment to Barbara Dunlop for her contribution to *The Highest Bidder* miniseries.

ISBN: 978 0 263 90073 6

Barbara Dunlop writes romantic stories while curled up in a log cabin in Canada's far north, where bears outnumber people and it snows six months of the year. Fortunately she has a brawny husband and two teenage children to haul firewood and clear the driveway while she sips cocoa and muses about her upcoming chapters. Barbara loves to hear from readers. You can contact her through her website: www.barbaradunlop.com

Recent titles by the same author:

AN INTIMATE BARGAIN
A COWBOY IN MANHATTAN
A COWBOY COMES HOME
AN AFTER-HOURS AFFAIR

Did you know these are also available as eBooks?
Visit www.millsandboon.co.uk

To my husband

One

Ann Richardson supposed she should be grateful the Interpol agents hadn't strip-searched her and slapped on the handcuffs. But after her sixth hour in the small, stuffy, gray-walled Federal Plaza interrogation room, she couldn't muster up anything but annoyance.

Agent Heidi Shaw was back, a half-filled cardboard coffee cup in one hand, clipboard tucked under her opposite arm with a sheaf of papers Ann assumed were some kind of investigative notes. Agent Shaw was playing bad cop to Agent Fitz Lydall's good. She was five feet even, maybe one hundred pounds soaking wet. While Fitz was two-twenty of solid muscle with a face like a bulldog and the shoulders of a linebacker. Privately, Ann thought the roles should be reversed, but she hadn't offered up that suggestion.

Either way, since she'd watched a few detective dramas in her time, it was easy enough to see through their textbook ploy. The fact that she was innocent was also going to mess with their strategy. Psychological tricks and circular questioning were not going to trip Ann up and make her tell them she was selling a stolen antique statue on behalf of her employer, Waverly's Auction House.

She'd learned a lot about Rayas's *Gold Heart* statues in the past few months. Three statues had been commissioned by King Hazim Bajal in the 1700s. They were said to bring luck in love to his daughters, who'd been required to marry for the convenience of their royal line and their country. One of the statues was still safe in Rayas with a modern branch of the Bajal family. The other had been lost at sea when the *Titanic* sank. A third had been stolen five months ago from another branch of the Rayasian royal family, the one that included Crown Prince Raif Khouri. Prince Raif was convinced Roark Black had stolen the statue on behalf of Waverly's. The accusation was preposterous. But the crown prince was a powerful, determined man, and he had both Interpol and the FBI dancing to his tune.

Heidi set her clipboard on the scarred wood table, and scraped back the metal folding chair to sit across from Ann. "Tell me about Dalton Rothschild."

"You don't read the tabloids?" Ann countered, giving herself a moment to consider this new line of questioning. Dalton was the CEO of Waverly's rival, Rothschild's.

"I understand the two of you were close."

"We were friends." Ann paused. "*Were* being the operative word." She'd never forgive Dalton for betraying her and destroying her professional reputation. His lies about their supposed affair were one thing. But his attack on her integrity was at a whole other level.

"Friends?" Heidi mocked with obvious skepticism and disdain.

"So, you do read the tabloids."

"I read everything. So I know you never denied he was your lover."

"Would you like me to deny it?"

"I'd like you to answer the question."

"I just did," Ann pointed out.

"Why are you being evasive?"

Ann shifted her body on the hard metal chair. She was being honest, not evasive, and she resented the agent's new barrage of questions. She articulated her next words slowly and carefully. "We were friends. He lied about me. We are no longer friends."

Heidi stood.

Ann longed to do the same. But every time she'd tried to rise from the uncomfortable chair, someone had brusquely ordered her to sit back down. Her legs were starting to cramp from inactivity, and her butt was killing her.

"Where's the statue?" Heidi fired at her.

"I don't know."

"Where's Roark Black?"

"I have no idea."

"He works for you."

"He works for Waverly's."

Heidi smirked. "Semantics."

"'I don't know where he is,' is not semantics. It's a statement of fact."

"You do know it's illegal to lie to Interpol."

"You do know I'm capable of calling a reporter at the *New York Times*."

Heidi braced her hands on the table, making triangles out of her thumbs and forefingers, and leaned forward. "Is that a threat?"

Ann realized her nerves were getting frayed, and her temper was starting to boil. She allowed for the possibility that she was no longer acting in her own best interest. "I'd like to call my lawyer."

"Guilty people say that all the time."

"So do women who've been denied a restroom for five hours."

Heidi's expression turned smug. "I can hold you for twenty-four hours without charging you."

"And without a restroom?" Ann taunted.

"You think this is a *joke?*"

"I think this is ridiculous. I've answered every question six times over. I have complete faith in Roark Black. There are two statues at play here. And Waverly's is *absolutely not* trading in stolen antiquities."

"So, you raised the *Titanic?*"

"I don't know the whys and the hows of where he got it, I only know Roark has the missing statue, not the stolen one."

Roark had also signed a confidentiality agreement with the mysterious owner of the *Gold Heart* statue that had gone missing one hundred years ago. He'd destroy his own career and compromise Waverly's reputation if he revealed the person's identity to anyone, including Ann.

"Where's the proof?" Heidi demanded.

"Where's my lawyer?" Ann shot back.

Heidi drew a breath and rose to full height. "You really want to go that route?"

Ann was out of patience. She was through being cooperative, through measuring her words. She was innocent, and nothing anybody said or did would alter that fact. "You really want a long and productive career in law enforcement?"

Heidi's brows shot up.

"Then start looking for a new suspect," said Ann. "Because it's not me, and it's not Roark. Maybe it is Dalton. Heaven knows he's the guy with a motive to discredit Waverly's. But if it is him, he's done it without my knowledge and certainly without my cooperation. I'm about to stop talking, Agent Shaw, and there's not a single thing you can do to make me say more. You want to be the hero, solve the big, international case, get promoted? Then *stop focusing on me.*"

Heidi paused for a beat. "You're an eloquent speaker."

Ann felt like she ought to say thank-you, but she kept her lips pressed tightly together.

"Then again, most liars are," Heidi finished.

Ann folded her hand on the table in front of her. She'd requested a restroom, and she'd requested a lawyer. If they were going to deny her requests, tromp all over her civil rights, she really would take the story to the *New York Times*.

Crown Prince Raif Khouri was completely out of patience. He didn't know how investigations were conducted in America, but in his own country of Rayas, Ann Richardson would have been thrown in jail by now. Let her spend a few nights in the bowels of Traitor's Prison; she'd be begging for an opportunity to confess.

He should have kept her in Rayas when she'd showed up there last month. Though he supposed canceling her visa and locking her up might have caused an international incident. And, at the time, he had been as anxious to get rid of her as she was to leave.

"Your Royal Highness?" A voice came over the intercom of the Gulfstream. "We'll be landing at Teterboro in a few minutes."

"Thank you, Hari," Raif responded. He straightened in the white leather seat, stretching the circulation back into his legs.

"I can show you the town while we're here," said Raif's cousin Tariq, gazing out his own window at the Manhattan skyline. Tariq had spent three years at Harvard, coming away with a law degree.

Raif's father, King Safwah, believed that an international education for the extended royal family would strengthen Rayas. Raif himself had spent two years at Oxford, studying history and politics. He'd visited many countries in Europe and Asia, but this was his first trip to America.

"We're not here to do the town," he pointed out to Tariq.

Tariq responded with a lascivious grin and a quirk of his dark brows. "American woman are not like Rayasian women."

"We're not here to chase women." Well, not plural anyway. They were here to chase and catch one particular woman. And then Raif was going to make her talk.

"There's this one restaurant that overlooks Central Park, and—"

"You want me to send you home?" Raif demanded.

"I want you to lighten up." Tariq was Raif's third cousin, but still an important player in the Rayasian royal circle. It gave him the right to be more forthright than others when speaking to Raif. But only to a point.

"We're here to find the *Gold Heart* statue," Raif stated firmly.

"We have to eat."

"We have to focus."

"And we'll do that a whole lot better with sustenance, such as maple glazed salmon and matsutake mushrooms."

"You should have been a litigator," Raif grumbled, fastening his seat belt as the landing gear whined then clunked into place. The two men had been friends since childhood, and he doubted he'd ever beaten Tariq in an argument.

Tariq leaned his head back in his seat, bracing himself for the landing. "I would have been a litigator. But the king objected."

"When I am king, you'll never be a litigator."

"When you are king, I am seeking asylum in Dubai."

Both men fought grins.

"Unless I can get you to lighten up," Tariq finished. "Maybe get you a girl."

"I can get my own girls." Raif needed to be discreet, of course, but he was no fan of celibacy.

The wheels of the Gulfstream touched smoothly onto the runway, its brakes engaging as they sped through the blowing December snow. He would never understand how such a pivotal city had grown up in a place with such appalling weather.

"There's this club off Fifth Avenue," said Tariq.

"I'm not in New York to get girls."

Even as he spoke, Raif couldn't seem to stop his thoughts from drifting to Ann Richardson. He'd been a fool to kiss her, a bigger fool to like it. And he'd been a colossal fool to let their single kiss get so far out of hand.

When he closed his eyes at night, he could still see her

wispy blond hair, that delicate, creamy skin, and her startling blue eyes. He could taste her hot, sweet lips and smell her vanilla perfume.

The Gulfstream slowed and turned, and finally rolled to a stop inside an airport hangar. The ground crew closed the huge door behind them against the cold weather.

When the airplane hatch opened, Raif and Tariq descended the small staircase. A few sounds echoed in the cavernous building—the door clanging into place, a heater whirring in the high ceiling and the ground crew calling to each other in the far corners. Beside the airplane, Raif and Tariq were greeted by the Rayasian ambassador, a couple of aides and some security staff.

Raif appreciated the low-key reception. He knew it was only a matter of time before his every trip would become a state occasion. Though still in his mid-sixties, his father had been ill for some time with the remnants of a tropical disease contracted decades ago in central Africa. These past few months had been hard on the king, and Raif was becoming more worried by the day that his father might not recover this time.

"Your Royal Highness." The ambassador greeted him with a formal bow. He was dressed in the traditional white robe of Rayas, his gray hair partially covered in a white cap.

Raif detected a slight narrowing of the ambassador's eyes as he took in Raif's Western suit.

But the man kept his thoughts to himself. "Welcome to America" was all he added.

"Thank you, Fariol." Raif shook the man's hand, rather than embracing him and air kissing as was the Rayasian custom. "You've arranged for a car?"

"Of course." Fariol gestured to a stretch Hummer limousine.

Raif raised a brow. "I believe my office said nondescript."

Fariol frowned. "There are no flags, no royal seals on the doors, no Rayasian markings whatsoever."

Raif heard Tariq shift beside him and guessed he was covering a smirk.

"I meant I wanted a sedan. Something plain and inconspicuous. Maybe something I could drive myself."

Fariol drew back in obvious confusion. The younger aide beside him stepped up to speak in his ear. "I can arrange it right away, Mr. Ambassador."

"Please do," Raif said directly to the aide, earning himself another censorious expression from the ambassador.

The aide nodded and quickly withdrew, pulling a phone from his pocket.

Fariol turned his attention away from Raif. "Sheik Tariq," he said.

It was a slight but very intentional snub. It was the crown prince who ended a conversation, not an ambassador.

Tariq gave Raif a fleeting, meaningful glance, silently acknowledging the break in protocol before responding. "Mr. Ambassador. Thank you for welcoming us."

"Do you know when you'll be returning to Rayas?"

Tariq paused for half a second, putting on an exaggerated expression of surprise. "When the crown prince decides it's time for us to leave America, of course."

The answer was an obvious rebuke of Fariol's attitude, and Raif had to suppress his own grin. Tariq might be overly familiar and opinionated in private. But in front of others, he paid strict adherence to the Rayasian royal hierarchy.

The aide rushed back. "Your car will be here in just a few minutes. A Mercedes sedan. S-Class. I hope that will please Your Royal Highness."

"That will be fine," Raif answered. He turned to Tariq. "Think you can get that address?"

Tariq looked to one of the security guards. "Jordan?"

The man stepped forward. "We're good to go, sir."

Jordan Jones was an American security specialist who'd become friends with Tariq after they met at Harvard. Raif had never met Jordan in person before, but he'd heard stories over the years that gave him a good deal of confidence in the man's abilities.

The bay door clattered partway open, and a steel-gray Mercedes sedan drove inside. Instantly, the flight crew appeared with the royal party's luggage, waiting as the vehicle came to a halt in front of Raif.

"That will be all, Fariol." Raif dismissed the ambassador with a curt nod, striding around the front of the car. Tariq and Jordan immediately fell into step.

"I'll drive." Raif held out his hand for the keys as a man appeared from the driver's seat.

"Sir?" Jordan prompted, arching a brow in Tariq's direction.

Glancing over his shoulder, presumably to ensure Fariol and his staff were out of earshot, Tariq spoke in a low tone. "You don't want to drive, Raif."

"Yes, I do."

"No, you don't."

The driver glanced from one man to the other. He was American, an employee of the rental company. In Rayas, there would have been no hesitation about who would win the argument. Raif's word there was law.

"Who's the prince around here?" Raif demanded of Tariq.

"Which one of us has driven in Manhattan?" Tariq countered.

"I'll drive," Jordan put in, deftly scooping the keys from the driver. He kept moving right past the surprised American, opening the back door of the sedan, turning to meet Raif's eyes. "Foreign royalty in the back. Brooklyn native at the wheel."

"You're pretty cocky," Raif said to Jordan.

"You know it…sir."

Raif followed Tariq to the backseat door. "In my country, I could have you beheaded," Raif lied.

"In my country, I could abandon you in Washington Heights." Jordan paused. "Same thing, really."

Raif couldn't help but grin as he got into the car. He didn't have a problem with people speaking truth to power, so long as they did it respectfully or in private. He was willing to concede that a born and raised New Yorker could probably get them to Ann Richardson's apartment faster than he could.

Jordan closed the back door of the car and then folded his big body into the driver's seat as the trunk clicked shut on their luggage.

"I understand you're at the Plaza," he said, adjusting the rearview mirror. "Their service is impeccable, and their security is tight."

"Nobody knows I'm here," said Raif. Security wasn't going to be an issue on the trip.

"Interpol knows you're here," Jordan responded. "Your passport sends off sirens and flashing lights in their Manhattan office."

Tariq chuckled.

"So does yours," Jordan warned Tariq.

"Interpol's got nothing against me," said Raif.

"They'll worry someone else does."

"The only person in America with something against me is Ann Richardson. And that's because I'm about to out her as a criminal and a liar."

Jordan pulled the car smoothly ahead, turning for the open bay door. "Interpol will watch you, and others watch Interpol." He straightened the wheel. "If there's anything happening in Rayas I should know about, political dissent, difficulties with neighboring countries, now would be the time to tell me."

"Some internal stuff," Tariq said. "Raif's uncle was stood up at the altar, as was a distant cousin Aimee. The *Gold Heart* statue theft is the only international scandal Rayas has had lately."

"I hear your father is ill," Jordan said to Raif, glancing at him in the rearview mirror.

"He's getting better," Raif said automatically.

"The truth doesn't matter, perception does. The perception is that your father is dying. And that means you're about to become king. And that means somebody, somewhere out there, wants to kill you."

"Just on general principle?" But Raif knew it was true.

"As a power play. Your cousin Kalila's next in line?"

"Yes."

"Who's close to her, especially lately?"

"You do know I'm only going to be here a few days," Raif said to Jordan. The man had been hired as temporary tour guide, not as the new head of Raif's security team.

"I still need to know the landscape."

"She's picked up a British boyfriend," said Tariq. "He's new."

Raif shot Tariq a glare. They didn't need to air the family laundry in front of Jordan. That Kalila had taken up with a completely unsuitable college boy instead of pledging her honor to a sheik's son in a neighboring country, as had been arranged a decade ago, was an embarrassment to the royal family. It was yet another thing upsetting the king. But it wasn't a matter of national security.

"His name?" asked Jordan, turning on the wipers as they drove into the snowstorm.

Raif interrupted. "You're driving us to Ann Richardson's, not compiling a family dossier."

"Niles," said Tariq. "That's all we've managed to get out of the stubborn girl. Kalila was the first casualty of the curse. And now Mallik's been jilted."

Raif gave an eye roll. "There is no curse."

"The curse of the *Gold Heart* statue?" asked Jordan.

"It's a foolish myth," said Raif, growing impatient. He was a tolerant man, but even he had his breaking point.

"This Niles guy?" Jordan asked. "He arrive out of nowhere?"

"He's a student," said Tariq.

"Of Arab descent?"

"Of very British descent." Raif switched to his most imperious voice, ending the conversation. "Let's stick to the mission, shall we? While we're in New York, Ann Richardson is our priority."

"Did you *see* this?" asked Ann's neighbor Darby Mersey, coming out her door and into the apartment hallway to follow Ann to her apartment.

Ann loved Darby dearly, but she really wanted to be alone tonight. After her ordeal with Interpol, all she could think about was a long, hot shower, a cup of herbal tea and about twelve hours of unconsciousness.

"See what?" she asked, praying the answer was short and succinct. She dropped her purse on the side table in the compact foyer and tossed her keys into the ceramic bowl as the apartment door closed behind them.

"Today's *Inquisitor*."

"I've been tied up all day long."

"Did you not walk past a newsstand? It's on the front page."

"What's on the front page?"

Judging by Darby's tone, Ann was not going to like the front page. And the very last thing she needed today was something more to worry about. Tomorrow. She could deal with more trouble tomorrow, once she'd had a chance to recover and regroup.

"Your picture."

Ann heaved a heavy sigh. She made her way toward the kitchen, deciding on a midpriced Cabernet Sauvignon instead of tea. Both would put her to sleep, but the wine would also help her stop fretting about what a mess her life had become.

"What's the scoop this week?" she asked.

She'd been a tabloid target many times before. The papers had a field day when Dalton Rothschild lied about having an affair with her. Reaction and speculation had swung from scandal to collusion. None of it had been true.

"'Turnabout seems to be fair play in the high-end auction world,'" Darby read as she followed along behind Ann.

"Now, there's a scoop," scoffed Ann as she snagged a bottle from her wine rack. She headed farther into the kitchen in search of a corkscrew. "What's next? 'Sale goes to the highest bidder'?"

Darby plopped herself on a wooden stool at the breakfast bar, spreading the tabloid newspaper on the counter in front of her.

"'Unable to clear either her own or her firm's name in the *Gold Heart* statue scandal, Ann Richardson seems to have decided to go the old-fashioned route.'"

Ann peeled the wrapper from the top of the bottle. "What's the old-fashioned route?"

"Sleeping her way out of trouble."

"With Dalton?" Ann wasn't quite following the reporter's logic on this. They'd been writing about her and Dalton for months. Talk about old news.

"With Prince Raif Khouri."

Ann froze, corkscrew poised. *"What?"*

"You heard me."

"That's a new low, even for them."

"They have a picture of you," Darby continued.

"So what?" They had several hundred pictures of Ann. Her personal favorite was the one taken in front of the Met as she was spilling her coffee all over her blouse.

"In this one, you're kissing the prince."

Ann felt the blood drain away from her face.

"It doesn't look like Photoshop."

Ann's stomach contracted to a ball of lead. There was only one time, only one way...

She made her way around the breakfast bar.

"Damn it." There she was, in grainy newsprint, her arms wrapped around Raif's neck, their lips locked together, her body bent slightly backward.

"Telephoto lens?" asked Darby.

"I was in Rayas." Who kept an eye out for tabloid reporters in Rayas?

"So, it's true?" Darby face lit up in a lascivious smile. "You slept with Prince Raif?"

"Of course it's not true." Ann paused. "I kissed him, obviously."

Darby was right. Photoshop was only so sophisticated. This was the real thing, and there was no point in denying it.

"But kissing was all we did," Ann continued. "And it was once. *One time*. Halfway around the world, for goodness' sake. In a private, walled garden at Valhan Palace."

For a fleeting moment, her memory swirled around that mind-blowing kiss on her last day, her last hour in Rayas. Not that she hadn't already relived it a thousand times.

"You didn't tell me you'd fallen for him," said Darby.

"I didn't fall for him. He's an arrogant jerk who thinks I'm a criminal and a liar."

Darby took in the picture again. "That's quite the kiss for an arrogant jerk."

"I'm not kissing him." Ann did lie this time. "He's kissing me."

Raif might have started the kiss, but it had become mutual in a heartbeat.

"So, he fell for you?" Darby looked as if she was mulling the possibilities.

"It wasn't a romantic kiss," Ann continued her explanation. "It was power play, a dominance thing. He was making a point."

Darby gave a sly smile this time. "Was the point that he was sexy?" She cocked her head, staring down at the picture again. "You sure don't look like you're fighting back."

Ann had to agree, and that was very unfortunate. Truth was, she hadn't been fighting back at all. Raif might be stubborn and arrogant, but he was definitely sexy. And he was one heck of a kisser. And there was no denying something had combusted between them the minute their lips touched. But Darby didn't need to know that.

Ann was busy forgetting all about it herself. "He was

making the point that in his country he could do anything he pleased, and I couldn't lift a finger to stop him. I got on the next plane."

Darby lifted her head. "Like what?"

"What, what?"

"You said he could do anything he pleased. Like what?"

Ann shrugged, moving back to the bottle of wine. She needed it now more than ever. "Like tax the poor, seize private property, nationalize an industry or throw the innocent in jail."

"He was going to throw you in jail?"

Ann popped out the cork, meeting Darby's eyes. "I wasn't completely sure."

"He kissed you instead?"

"I think so. And I don't think he expected to like it. It threw him for a minute, and it gave me a chance to escape."

Darby stretched up to pull two wineglasses from the hanging rack at the end of the breakfast bar. "Why didn't you tell me any of this?"

"Denial works better if you're not dissecting the nuances with your best friend."

Darby set down the glasses. "Too bad for you that there's photographic evidence."

Ann allowed her gaze to move to the picture. Denial wasn't working all that well anyway. She could still feel his strong arms around her, taste his hot lips on hers, smell the spicy scent of the Rayasian night and feel the ocean breeze rustle her hair. A tingle ran through her body at the vivid memory.

"Better fill these up," Darby's voice interrupted as she pushed the two glasses toward Ann.

Ann wholeheartedly agreed.

But before she could pour, the apartment buzzer interrupted her. They both glanced toward it.

"Don't answer," Darby advised. "It could be a reporter."

Ann agreed. Then again, it could be Edwina. Ann's cell phone had been off most of the day, and elderly Waverly's board member Edwina Burrows had a habit of dropping by in the early evening if she was out walking her cocker spaniel.

Ann needed to tell Edwina about the Interpol interview. She also needed to explain about the picture of her and Prince Raif. Edwina was one of Ann's strongest supporters on the Waverly's board of directors, and right now Ann needed all the help she could get.

"It could be Edwina," she told Darby, crossing to the speaker. She wiped her sweaty palms along her thighs. If it was a reporter, she'd simply lie and say Ann Richardson wasn't home and wouldn't be back for the foreseeable future. "Hello?"

"Ann? This is Prince Raif Khouri," said a man in what was obviously a fake Rayasian accent. "We need to talk."

"Right," Ann scoffed into the speaker, shaking her head in Darby's direction. It wasn't exactly a sophisticated con. "Tell your editor it didn't work."

Darby helpfully filled the two wineglasses.

"I don't know what you meant by that, Ann," said the voice. "But I've come a long way for this conversation."

Actually, the accent wasn't bad. Points to the *Inquisitor* for having found a Rayasian to use as a stringer.

Ann pressed the button again. "Have I done something to make you people think I'm stupid?"

"Don't say anything!" Darby hissed as she walked into the living room. "They'll quote you."

The voice crackled through the speaker, deeper and more imperious this time. "Ms. Richardson, have I done something to make you think there is any chance in the world I will give up?"

As the deep tone hit her nervous system, Ann's pulse leaped. She recognized that voice. She was afraid of that voice. And, heaven help her, she was aroused by that voice.

Darby blinked at Ann's stunned expression. "What?"

Ann swallowed against her suddenly dry throat. "It's him."

It took Darby a beat to respond. "Him, him?"

Ann nodded.

"Prince *Raif?*"

Ann's nod slowed. Raif was in America. And he knew where she lived.

"Step away from the intercom," Darby advised in an undertone, moving closer for support.

Ann snapped her hand from the button and took a step back.

"Don't let him in," Darby whispered.

Ann nearly laughed at the absurdity of the advice. She sure didn't need Darby to warn her off Raif. She took one of the glasses of wine, gulping a swallow as she stepped farther away from the intercom. "Not in a million years."

Two

Raif had never understood the American obsession over what was legal versus what was logical. But he'd acquiesced to Tariq and Jordan's advice about stalking laws and waited twenty-four hours until he could approach Ann "legitimately" at a charity event.

Since it had once been a family home, the building was a multitude of rooms and hallways spread over several floors. For the evening's event, each room had been decorated thematically for a different European country, featuring festive cuisine and drinks to match the decor. Raif wasn't interested in eating or drinking, nor was he interested in mingling. On arrival, he'd made a generous donation on behalf of the royal family, was introduced to the chairman of the hospital board, complimented the chairman's wife's dress, then moved on his way, searching for Ann.

The hospital fund-raiser was taking place at the Crystal Sky Restaurant, a historic building that had originally been built as an industrialist's mansion in the 1930s. It was characterized by floor-to-ceiling glass walls, overlooking extensive grounds, which were now decorated for the Christmas season.

He finally spotted Ann in the Swedish room. She was next to a giant reindeer, partially obscured by a lattice wall of colorful, shining stars. He stopped for a moment. The scents of chocolate and nutmeg surrounded him, and Ann filled his vision.

He left the German room, with its boisterous carols, evergreen boughs and carved wooden towns, moving down a hallway to France, which featured berry-festooned wreaths, delicate angels and yards of spun glass. Someone tried to hand him a glass of champagne, but he politely declined and moved on.

She was stunningly beautiful in a dramatic red strapless ball gown. It was tight across her breasts, fitted along her waist, accented with a band of clear crystals that dropped to a large crystal brooch at her hip. The skirt fell in soft folds of shimmering satin, down to the floor, where a glittering red strappy sandal was visible beneath the hem.

She laughed with the man standing next to her. Then she took a sip of champagne. Her red lips touched the rim of the glass, reminding Raif of the moment he'd kissed her. A shot of arousal coursed through him, but he ruthlessly tamped it down. He put his feet in motion, making his way across the crowded floor.

He was offered eggnog this time, by a tuxedoed waiter holding a tray of cut-crystal glasses. Again, he declined, sights set on his target. Ann took her leave of the other man, moving out into the open. Raif was twenty feet away when she recognized him. Her crystal-blue eyes widened, and her lips parted in obvious surprise.

He was five feet away when her surprise turned to annoyance.

"Go away," she hissed at him.

"We need to talk."

"Not in public, we don't."

"Then let's go somewhere private." He'd prefer that anyway.

"Walk away, Raif. I am not giving the *Inquisitor* another photo op." Her gaze darted worriedly to the people around them.

"Who said anything about a picture?"

"You must have seen the *Inquisitor.*"

In fact, Jordan had brought it to his attention yesterday. "I don't read the tabloids."

"Neither do I," Ann responded tartly. "And I'm not planning to be their feature again either."

"Good thing I wasn't planning to kiss you."

She shot him a glare, moving around him. "We can't be seen together."

He grasped her bare arm. "Oh, no, you don't."

"Let go of me," she demanded.

"Not until we talk."

"You're hurting me."

"No, I'm not." His grip wasn't nearly as tight as he'd like it to be.

She might be paranoid about the press, but he didn't particularly care who saw them together. And he didn't care if the world accused them of having an affair. He wasn't going to let public opinion dictate his actions.

"Are you trying to ruin my life?" she demanded.

"Are you trying to ruin mine?"

"I had nothing to do with your statue being stolen."

"So you've claimed." He didn't believe her, not for one minute. In fact, he was insulted that she thought he might. New information had come to light, including his uncle Prince Mallik's description of the thief. The man who'd broken into the palace had a voice similar to Roark Black's.

"Raif, please. Not here. Not now." Her pleading words caused an unwelcome and unfamiliar surge of sympathy inside him.

He fought it. He owed this woman no consideration whatsoever. But something in her clear blue eyes made him weak.

Hating himself, he eased her behind the star-festooned screen to give them some privacy.

"That help?" he asked.

"No," she grated.

There was a door in the wall next to them. She wanted privacy? Fine. He twisted the knob, pushing it open and swiftly spiriting her inside.

"Hey," she protested as he closed the door. "You can't—"

"I just did." He shut the door behind them, and his eyes adjusted to the gloom. A woman should be careful what she asked for.

They'd entered a small, private dining area. A single table for six sat in the center of the room. Wine racks lined the two inside walls, while the two outside walls were dominated by bay windows that looked over the sloping gardens all decorated with colored lights.

Ann started for the door. "Let me out of here."

Raif moved to block her exit. "No one will see us here," he offered with a trace of sarcasm.

"That's not the point."

"What is the point, Ann? That when I'm standing in front of you demanding answers, you can't keep up your pretense forever?"

Her jaw clenched as she glared up at him. The sounds of an a cappella quartet wafted through the walls, along with the murmur of conversation and the occasional spurt of laughter.

"It's not a pretense," she finally said.

He searched her expression for dishonesty, but instead found himself drinking in her beauty. Memories surged, and he wanted to touch her smooth cheeks, run his hands over her bare shoulders, taste her delicate skin and her dark, sexy lips.

"Ann," he breathed.

Then anger unexpectedly left her voice, replaced by what sounded like weariness. "What is it you want me to say, Raif?"

It wasn't what he wanted her to say. It was what he wanted

her to do. And what he wanted her to do had nothing whatsoever to do with his family's statue.

"How can I end this?" she asked.

"Give me my statue." He forcibly pulled his thoughts back
from the brink.

"That's impossible."

"Then tell me where it is."

"I don't know where it is."

"Then bring me Roark Black."

"Roark doesn't have your statue."

Raif took a step closer, crowding her, determined to get
this farce over with. "In Rayas, we would not ask so politely."

She sucked in a small breath, but mulishly pursed her lips.

Raif clenched his fists against the desire to kiss her.

"We're not in Rayas," she told him.

"Pity," he found himself responding. There was enough
of the modern world in him that he'd never take an unwilling
woman to bed. But there was enough tradition in him that he
wished he could do it with Ann.

"Why?" she asked. "If we were in Rayas, would you throw
me in a dungeon?" Her irises were opaque in the glow of
Christmas lights filtering through the bay windows.

He decided to be honest. "If we were in Rayas, I'd tie you
to my bed."

Her eyes went wide at his blunt words, and her jaw dropped
a notch.

"A hundred years ago," he continued, letting his fantasies
roam free, "I would have tied you to my bed the night you
kissed me."

"Lucky for me times have changed. And it was you who
kissed me."

"Maybe." He let his gaze do a sweep of her sexy body. "But
I could have kept you happy in my bed."

"Does your ego know no bounds?"

"I'm told I'm an excellent lover."

She crossed her arms over her chest, and it had the unfortunate result of highlighting her cleavage. "By women you can have thrown in a dungeon?"

"Mostly," he allowed with a shrug, struggling to tear his gaze from her breasts. It had never occurred to him to care that his lovers might be humoring him.

"You should try it someday with someone over whom you don't have the power of life and death."

"Thanks for the advice." He wanted that someone to be Ann. Right here, right now.

"See if you still get a gold star then," she continued to taunt him.

"Unless you're volunteering for the job, I suggest we change the subject."

"What?"

He raised his brows and pinned her with a smoldering, meaningful stare.

She swallowed. "Oh."

"Yes."

Her arms shifted so that she was hugging herself. "I didn't mean…"

"My father is gravely ill." Raif ruthlessly changed the subject. "The missing *Gold Heart* statue has caused him much distress."

Ann's voice became small. "I'm very sorry to hear that."

Raif's chest went unexpectedly tight. He had to struggle to keep the emotion from his voice. It was odd. He talked about his father all the time without reaction. "The statue's return would give the king peace of mind."

Ann touched Raif's arm. "I would if I could."

His gaze went to her pale, delicate hand, then lifted to her face. Her expression was open, honest and compassionate. It was difficult to believe she was a thief.

"Then do it," he rasped.

"I can't." Her eyes took on a sheen of tears.

His arm snaked around her waist, and he leaned down. "But, you can."

"Raif…" Her soft voice trailed away.

Her lithe body was warm against his. Her curves molded to his angles. A throbbing pulse moved inexorably through his body, as her lavender perfume teased his senses.

He was going to kiss her.

He was going to kiss her again, and there was no force on earth that could stop him.

He anchored her head with his hand, reveling in the feel of her wispy blond hair. He leaned in, anticipating the sweet taste of her hot lips.

"California," she gasped.

He halted. "What?"

"Roark said he was going to California."

Raif forced himself to ease back. "You're going to have to be a lot more specific than that."

"Los Angeles." She struggled against his hold. "He usually stays at the Santa Monica Reginald."

"You're lying."

She shook her head.

"You're giving me Roark."

"Yes."

"To avoid a kiss."

"The last one got me into quite a lot of trouble."

Raif let his hand slide from her soft hair. Their last kiss had put him in a whole lot of trouble of a different kind. He couldn't get her out of his head, and his attraction to her was messing with his focus on the good of his country.

"Santa Monica?"

She nodded, eyes clear, gaze direct. "The Reginald."

"And, he has the statue?"

"He'll tell you all about it."

Raif hesitated. "That was too easy."

"It wasn't remotely easy for me."

Again, he gauged her expression.

"Let go of me, Raif. Assault is a crime in this country."

"I'm not hurting you."

"You need my permission to hold me like this."

"That's ridiculous."

"Maybe in Rayas. But here, what you've done is also kidnapping and forcible confinement."

"I moved you maybe five feet."

"You won't let me leave."

He knew she was blowing things way out of proportion. Still, she'd given him something. He ought to let her go now.

He eased his arm from around her back, and she immediately scooted away.

"You're free to go," he told her.

"How magnanimous of you." Her voice was confident, but she wasted no time moving out of his reach and over to the exit. She opened the door and walked out without glancing back.

For a moment, Raif worried that he'd truly frightened her. But she had to know she was physically safe. He might have kissed her, but that was all. He certainly would never have harmed her.

Then he gave himself a mental shake. She was a thief who was hurting his family. If he'd made her a little nervous, she'd brought it on herself. Her admission proved he'd been right about her all along.

He was heading for California now, and he was about to make Roark Black more than a little nervous.

"Does nothing scare you?" asked Darby as she swiped her sweaty, dark hair back off her forehead.

Side by side, the two women pedaled exercise bikes in a row of about thirty identical machines on the top floor of the Blackburn Gym. Ann was at mile eighteen, but she suspected Darby was in the lead. A muted news show played on screens in front of them, the closed-captioned words scrolling beneath. The reporter and a distinguished-looking gray-haired man were talking about shipping routes and cargo costs out of the Mediterranean.

"It's not like he'll know it was me," Ann responded reasonably, drawing deep breaths as she pedaled. "And it worked, didn't it?"

"That's short-term thinking," said Darby.

"I prepaid three nights at the Reginald hotel in Santa Monica in Roark's name," said Ann. "Raif and his henchmen will sleuth out the fact that he's registered there pretty quickly. Then they'll stake the building out, waiting for him to show up."

"And when the three nights are over?"

Ann shrugged. "Raif will assume Roark either caught on to the stakeout or had a change of plans. If I'm lucky, he'll hang around California awhile longer and keep looking for him."

"You sent the crown prince of Rayas on a wild goose chase."

"Well, I sure couldn't let him stay here and follow me around the city." Never mind the constant threat of the tabloid photographers catching them in the same frame somewhere, and her need to focus on the year-end auction happening tonight. Ann had been seconds away from kissing Raif at the fund-raiser. She couldn't go there, not ever again.

"Any luck in really finding Roark?"

Ann shook her head, pulling her damp T-shirt from her torso to circulate a bit of air. "I've left him a dozen messages. Either he's seriously out of touch, or he's afraid to respond to me."

"The FBI still after him?"

"They're still interested in him. So is Interpol, obviously. But without evidence of theft—" she gave Darby a hard look "—which they'll *never* find."

"Because he hid it so well, or because it doesn't exist?"

"It doesn't exist."

"You're positive."

"I've known Roark long enough to be positive. He may not be in touch at the moment, but he's out there trying to clear Waverly's name. I'd stake my life on it."

Roark engaged in a high-stakes, high-risk profession, but he was a man of principles and professionalism. He had assured Ann that his *Gold Heart* statue was legitimate, and she absolutely believed him. Though, on days like this, she wished he'd hurry up about proving it.

She watched the bike's digital odometer as it neared twenty miles.

"If you're wrong about Roark?" Darby asked quietly.

"Then I lose my job," Ann said, owning up to the worst-case scenario. "I'm disgraced in my profession. And Waverly's is likely the object of a hostile takeover by Rothschild's."

"Good thing the stakes aren't too high."

"Good thing."

Ann's readout hit twenty, and she stopped pedaling, breathing deep, her heart thumping in her chest. She snagged a white towel from the handlebars and rubbed the sweat from her forehead and the back of her neck.

Darby stopped pedaling, too. A quick glance at Darby's odometer told Ann her friend had made twenty-three miles. Ann had to be getting lazy.

"I have to get my butt home and get ready for work," she told Darby. "Big night tonight."

"What are you selling at the auction?" Darby climbed from the bike.

"It's my favorite sale of the year. Luxury items with killer provenance. They're for billionaires with last-minute Christmas lists," Ann joked, straightening her T-shirt over her yoga pants as she dismounted.

The Christmas season was Waverly's last chance each year to hit their annual sales targets. The focus of the auction tonight was estate jewelry and antique furniture from some notable families on both sides of the Atlantic. Waverly's had been in business long enough to know what wealthy men wanted to pick up for their wives and girlfriends in December.

Any old millionaire could buy a twenty-carat diamond bracelet, but few men had the real money it took to buy their loved ones jewelry once worn by European royalty. Provenance was everything in the auction business.

Ann bent down to shut off her bike.

"Uh-oh." Darby's tone was dire, her hand suddenly grasping the back of Ann's shoulder.

"What?" Ann straightened in confusion.

Darby nodded to the television screen.

Dalton Rothschild was speaking, but the closed-captioning didn't show his words. The picture of Ann kissing Raif flashed on the screen.

"Can you tell what he's saying?" Ann asked worriedly.

Black and white words finally came up on the bottom half of the screen.

Do you expect shareholders to accept Rothschild's offer? the reporter had asked.

Given the events of the past days, and Ms. Richardson's rapidly deteriorating credibility, Dalton had replied, *I expect the board to recommend it.*

"That son of a bitch," growled Darby.

"He does play dirty," Ann agreed, her mind scrambling to figure out what Dalton was talking about.

Had something changed? She was under no illusion that she had the unanimous support of the board. She'd guessed it was about fifty-fifty. Though, thanks to Raif, the balance might have tipped away from her yesterday.

But that didn't explain why they'd recommend shareholders sell to Rothschild's.

Then again, Dalton could easily be lying to the reporter about the board recommending the sale. At least, she hoped he was lying. If he wasn't lying, she might as well cash out her modest investments, find a cheap beach hut somewhere in the Caribbean and then call it retirement, because her professional life would be over.

"What are you going to do?" asked Darby, as the news channel switched to another story.

"I have to talk to Edwina." Ann flipped the towel over her shoulder and started toward the showers where her cell phone was secured in a locker. She needed to find out if it was true.

If so, she needed to know which board members were supporting Dalton.

"What about Roark?" Darby asked, falling into step.

Despite her brave front, Ann had been struggling for days now not to lose patience with Roark.

"I know it's complicated," she allowed. "But if he doesn't show up soon with the proof that we have the missing *Gold Heart* statue and not Raif's stolen one, he might as well not bother. There'll be no Waverly's left to sell it."

"Are they going to fire you?" Darby asked, as they left the noise of the exercise room behind and made their way down the wide hallway.

"I expect I'll find out after tonight's auction."

That was the bald truth of it. Some of the board members were intensely loyal and trusted her implicitly. They gave her full credit for the growth of the company over the past few years. Ann knew she'd done well, but she also knew she was rapidly becoming a liability.

"Damn you, Raif Khouri," she muttered between clenched teeth.

If the man hadn't been so insistent about the statue. If he hadn't lit a fire under the Interpol agents. If he hadn't accused her, or kissed her…

If it wasn't for Raif, she'd at least have a fighting chance at keeping her job.

Raif gazed out at the nighttime view of Manhattan from the royal suite at the Plaza Hotel. Anger had churned in the pit of his stomach since he'd discovered Ann's duplicity this morning. He'd wasted two days on a fool's errand. Roark wasn't in California. He'd probably never been in California. Sure, there was a reservation under his name in the hotel, but a little digging by Jordan had revealed the room had been charged to Ann's credit card.

Raif knew the woman was smart. Now he realized she was also cunning. Well, the gloves were off. He knew exactly where he stood, and he was going after her with no hesitation whatsoever.

He heard the suite door open, then close.

"It's done," said Tariq, his footsteps bringing him across the thick carpet to where Raif stood.

"She bought it?" Raif asked without turning.

"Ann will be here in twenty minutes."

"Good." Raif smiled to himself in grim satisfaction.

"You hungry?" asked Tariq.

"Not in the least."

"I thought maybe later—"

"I'll be busy later."

Tariq was still for a moment. "Do I want to ask?"

"No, you don't. Jordan left?"

"He did."

"You should go, too."

"Raif, you won't—"

Raif turned sharply. "Won't what?"

He could almost see the war going on inside Tariq's head. Did he dare treat Raif like a cousin and boyhood friend, and question his actions? Or was now a time to defer to Raif as the future king?

"You should go, too," Raif repeated softly.

"I worry about you," said Tariq.

"I worry about Rayas," Raif responded.

"You won't hurt her," Tariq dared to say.

"I don't know. She did what she did, and I need what I need." Raif honestly wasn't sure what he'd be willing to do to Ann. But he did know he didn't need to justify it to Tariq. He changed the subject. "Kalila called today."

"Has she come to her senses?" asked Tariq.

"Not in the least. She's a spoiled brat."

Raif's younger cousin couldn't seem to think of anything but her own selfish desires—not the king, and not her country.

"She's a product of her time," Tariq offered.

"I never should have let her go to school in Istanbul."

Tariq joined him at the window. "She needs to understand the world."

"She needs to understand her duty."

Tariq was silent for a moment. "You don't think it's the *Gold Heart* curse?"

"There is no curse."

Tariq paused for a thoughtful moment. "Then why are you falling for Ann Richardson?"

"I want to strangle Ann Richardson."

"You want to kiss her senseless first."

Raif didn't deny it. "That's got nothing to do with romance. It's lust."

There was no way Raif would give credence to the *Gold Heart* curse. Mallik's young fiancée had simply changed her mind, and his cousin Aimee was better off with her replacement groom, Jacx.

"You sure?"

"Completely." Raif was a healthy man, and Ann was a stunningly beautiful woman. There would be something wrong with him if he didn't want to ravish her. It had nothing to do with any missing statue.

"You step too far over the line, and they'll deport you," Tariq warned.

"I won't step over the line."

Tariq coughed out a laugh. "We're in America. You can't even see the line."

"I'll be fine. You should go. I don't want you getting any more caught up in this."

"Fine with me." Tariq stepped back. "I know a great little club on Fifth Avenue. Fine music, great cognac, gorgeous women. Don't wait up."

"I never do," Raif responded, his mind already moving on to what he'd say and do when Ann showed up.

The next sound he heard was Tariq leaving the suite and the whir of the private elevator as it descended.

He waited ten minutes, then moved to an alcove in the living room to wait for Ann, choosing a spot where he wasn't in the line of sight from the door.

A few minutes later, as planned, a butler showed her in, seating her at the main furniture grouping in the center of the large room. Raif waited until the butler left, and until she began glancing around with curiosity, before he stepped out of the shadows to reveal himself.

At his first movement, Ann came to her feet. "Hello. Mr. Oswald? I'm—"

"Hello, Ann." He moved toward her.

"Raif? What?" She glanced behind her. "I'm supposed to meet—"

"Leopold Oswald. Yes, I know."

The confusion grew on her face. "He's interested in auctioning some of his paintings."

Raif came to a halt in front of her. "I'm afraid not."

"Did he change his mind? Don't tell me you said something to him? Raif, you can't—"

"Think about it, Ann." He gave her a moment. "Leopold was never part of the equation."

She stopped, eyes narrowing. He could see her catching on.

"I was supposed to meet Roark," Raif helpfully added. "You were supposed to meet Leopold…." He waited for her to fill in the blanks.

"Leopold's not coming."

"Give the woman a gold star."

"You lied to me. Or somebody with a very convincing German accent lied to me."

"Just like you lied to me," he told her softly.

"I thought Roark would be in Santa Monica," she said, perpetuating the lie.

Raif scoffed his disbelief. "*You* booked the reservation. *You* paid for three nights at the hotel."

She gave up the pretense. "Okay, you weren't supposed to find out that part."

"No kidding."

"I had to get you out of my hair. This is a critical time for Waverly's, a critical time for my career."

"So, you're saying there can be times when it's justifiable to lie?"

"When you're in the right, yes."

"Good." He nodded. "Then you'll understand what I'm about to do."

She stilled, then took a half step back, suspicion evident in her tone. "What are you about to do?"

"I'm going to call Roark Black and offer to make a trade." He pulled out his phone. "Consider yourself kidnapped, Ann."

She blinked once, then a second time. "Don't be ridiculous."

Raif just smiled, while she obviously struggled to put the pieces together.

Predictably, she went for the suite door.

"There's a guard standing right outside. He's Rayasian. Very loyal to me."

She stumbled a step, but kept going, opening the door wide, coming face-to-face with six-foot-four, two-hundred-sixty-pound Ali Geensh. Ali scowled down at her.

Ann gave a little jump and quickly closed the door.

She scrambled in her purse for her cell phone.

In three strides, Raif was whisking it from her hands. "Thank you. I wasn't sure how I'd get hold of Roark's private number." Raif pressed a key on her phone. "I trust it's in your contact list?"

"Give that back." She tried to snatch it away.

He held it out of her reach. "Don't waste your effort."

"You have no right—"

"Neither did you. I flew all the way across the country, and then all the way back again. I think you lost the moral high ground three days ago, Ann."

"I didn't break any laws."

"That help you sleep better at night?"

"I sleep just fine."

"So will I." Raif scrolled through Ann's contact list, finding Roark's number. He pressed the dial button.

She frowned. "I've left him a dozen messages."

"Not like this you haven't," Raif responded as Roark's voice mail greeting played through.

"Roark," said Raif. "It's Prince Raif. I have Ann. Call me."

Her eyes went round. "They'll arrest you. Truly, Raif. This is really kidnapping."

"They won't arrest me." To start with, he had no intention of getting caught. He wanted the statue, and from what he'd read and heard, Roark would do what he had to do to save Ann.

"You're holding me hostage and *ransoming me*. How on earth do you expect this to end?"

"I expect to end with Roark bringing me my *Gold Heart*."

"Along with the SWAT team. Call him back, Raif. Shut this down. Let me go."

Raif shook his head. "You had your chance to do this the honest way."

"This is honest to God kidnapping, Raif. They'll throw you in jail for twenty years."

Raif scoffed. "At worst, they'll deport me. And since Rayas is one of the only politically stable sources of rare earth minerals, they'll get over my indiscretions awfully quick." He tucked her phone securely into his suit jacket pocket. "You haven't figured it out yet, have you?"

Her eyes narrowed in obvious confusion. "Figured out what?"

"Who I am. What I can do. I'm the crown prince of a foreign nation, Ann. I have diplomatic immunity. I can get away with anything."

She swallowed convulsively. "Diplomatic…"

He clicked his jaw in pity. "You're at my mercy now."

Three

"I'm not about to play this game with you, Raif." Ann thought seriously about sprinting for the hotel suite door, but she doubted the Rayasian sumo wrestler's mood had improved in the past five minutes.

"Who said anything about a game?" Raif asked evenly.

He looked frustratingly calm and at ease in the opulent surroundings. His dark suit was crisp and beautifully cut. His white shirt was flawless, and his geometric burgundy and steel-gray tie gave him an air of authority. She'd never seen a picture of him anything but perfectly shaved, and she had to wonder if a barber trimmed his hair every morning. She could only imagine the price of his black wingtips.

"Come on. You don't seriously expect me to believe you'll keep me here."

He shrugged. "You're here, aren't you?"

"I'm leaving."

"You're welcome to try." His expression was as level as his tone.

Watching him warily, she took a sideways step to the nearest hotel phone. She lifted the receiver. Silence. She pressed the zero key. It made a tone, but nothing else happened.

"You've disabled the phones?" she asked in disbelief.

Raif said nothing.

"Why do I get the feeling this isn't your first kidnapping?"

"It's the first time anyone's tried to escape."

"What?" she scoffed. "Your victims normally throw themselves panting at your feet?"

"It happens."

"You live in a bubble, you know that?"

"I'm aware that I'm living a privileged life."

"Privileged?" She smacked the receiver down into the cradle. "Privileged is a night nanny, your own bouncy castle and a Porsche for your sixteenth birthday. You're an insufferable little potentate who desperately needs somebody to set some boundaries."

His eyes narrowed. "And you're a conniving little hypocrite who desperately needs somebody to hook her up to a polygraph."

"You got one of those?" she taunted. "Because I'll take one, right here, right now."

"I have to admit, I didn't think of that." He looked regretful.

"Too bad. We could solve this whole problem right now."

"We'll solve the problem when Roark calls back."

"Roark's not going to call."

The last thing international man of mystery Roark Black would do was enter into negotiations with a kidnapper.

"I've got an auction tonight," Ann pointed out. "I have to go to work."

Raif held his palms up in a gesture of surrender. "You have to go to work? Why didn't you say something? In that case, I give up. You're free to go."

"Jerk," Ann muttered, huffing as she crossed her arms over her chest.

"Hungry?" he asked.

She was, but she sure wasn't about to admit it. There was

no way she was accepting any kindness from him. She'd read all about Stockholm syndrome.

"Not in the least," she answered tartly. But she did plunk herself down on the sofa. She'd been standing in too-tight three-inch heels since she left the gym this morning, and her feet were killing her.

She'd dressed to impress at tonight's auction, but she didn't give one whit what Raif thought of her. If she'd known this was going to happen, she'd have gone for a less fitted skirt, a less tailored blouse and jacket. And she sure wouldn't have worn this particular bra. It was brand-new, with underwires and stiff lace. Not her wisest purchase ever, but it had looked awfully good in the store.

"Are you always this stubborn?" he asked, taking the armchair at the end of the sofa.

"I'm sorry," she asked with false sweetness, "am I not behaving like a proper kidnap victim?"

He stretched his legs out, crossing his ankles. "All you have to do is cooperate, and this whole thing will be over before you know it."

"Just so you know, I know it already, and it's not over."

He twitched the tiniest of smiles. "Cooperate, Ann."

"By *cooperate,* you mean admit I stole your statue." She was getting sick and tired of people trying to get her to do that.

Raif pulled his phone out of his inside pocket and pressed a button. "Gold star for you," he offered before raising it to his ear. "Ali? Dinner for one."

Ann rolled her eyes.

"Change your mind?" Raif asked.

"No." She came to her feet. "Am I free to use the bathroom?"

"Go ahead." He nodded toward a wide hallway behind the grand piano.

Ann turned on her heel and marched across the big room. The bathroom was halfway down on the left. While at the end of the hall, double doors opened into a massive master bedroom, with a four-poster king-size bed covered in a hunter-green satin quilt.

She swallowed as she turned into the bathroom, banishing an image of herself in the bed with Raif.

He wouldn't.

That would be going way too far.

He might have diplomatic immunity, but she had to believe he had some kind of a moral code. At least she hoped he did. And she sure hoped it wasn't some weird Rayasian moral code that allowed him to have his way with any woman who happened to be available.

She closed the door behind her and firmly turned the lock, leaning against it and squeezing her eyes shut. She felt better locked inside the bathroom. It occurred to her that she could simply stay in here until Raif came to his senses.

She opened her eyes and gazed at herself in the lighted mirror. Staying in here wasn't a half-bad idea. The lock would keep Raif out. And if he wasn't standing in front of her, she could pretend she wasn't attracted to him.

She glanced around at her surroundings.

She was standing in the biggest bathroom she'd ever seen. A four-person tub was recessed into a frosted bay window. It was surrounded by leafy green plants and white candles, with a cushioned bench seat and a small table adjacent. There were his-and-hers sinks at opposite ends of a long marble counter. Fine toiletries were placed around the room in wicker baskets, and two plush robes hung on hooks on the wall.

The toilet was placed discreetly in a frosted-glass chamber, while a separate, huge shower stall featured a dozen nozzles along the walls and in the ceiling. There had to be ten towels, and a telephone....

Hello.

She crossed the room, lifting the slim ivory receiver. She held her breath and put it to her ear.

Silence.

"Darn."

She supposed that had been too much to hope for.

Her gaze strayed to the tub again. She rubbed the side of her rib cage where the tight bra was digging in and the lace scratched her skin. A long, hot bath would feel awfully good. And it would certainly serve Raif right to cool his heels out there without her.

If he expected her to get hysterical or collapse in a fit of despair, he was sorely mistaken. Diplomatic immunity or not, there were going to be consequences for his outrageous actions. Ann would make sure of that.

But until then, her options were limited. She could go back to the living room and try to reason with an obstinate jerk. Or she could go back and watch him dine on room service while she sat hungry. Or she could stay right here and take advantage of the hotel amenities.

"Take that, Raif Khouri," she mumbled.

She moved to the side of the tub, experimentally twisting one of the taps. Water instantly gushed out—hot, soothing water.

She flipped the lever to engage the plug.

But as the water bubbled up in the tub, she lost her nerve. Did she really want to get naked with Raif on the other side of the wall? Shouldn't she get back out there and plead her case one more time? If she didn't show up tonight, didn't call, didn't offer Waverly's any explanation, it would very likely push the board toward firing her.

Would Raif have any sympathy for her plight?

She tried to picture it and couldn't.

He'd simply tell her to confess to the theft, and he'd let her go. He'd like it that she was under additional pressure. It would play right into his hand.

She glanced back down at the water, wondering how long it would take for him to give up on the kidnapping plot. Overnight at least. Maybe even all of tomorrow.

Then she wondered what the police or FBI would do once her friends reported her missing. Would they look for her right away, or would they wait the official twenty-four hours? No-body knew she'd come to the Plaza tonight. And the Interpol agents might think she'd fled the city, or the state, or maybe even the country. There was every chance the law-enforcement officials would take her disappearance as confirmation of her guilt.

She perched on the edge of the tub, accepting the fact that the cavalry wasn't coming. Roark wasn't going to call. And there was no way Raif was going to listen to reason.

The water level in the tub continued to rise.

Ann slipped off her shoes, sighing as she wiggled her toes. Red indents had formed on her heels and on her baby toes. She fingered her way through the expensive toiletries on the tiled ledge beside her, finding a book of matches and a tiny bottle of lavender bath oil. Her favorite.

She unscrewed the cap, sniffing the contents. Nice.

She poured a dollop into the water and inhaled apprecia-tively. The aroma was very soothing.

She replaced the cap, set down the bottle and picked up a book of matches. She struck one, and lit the nearest candle, then another and another. The tub was nearly full, so she shut off the taps.

Throwing caution firmly to the wind, she stripped off her jacket, moving aside one of the thick bath towels to give her-self a place to hang it. She unbuttoned her blouse and shim-mied out of her skirt. Then she determinedly pulled off her slip and unsnapped the wicked bra.

As she shimmied out of her panties, her gaze caught on something under the vanity counter. A minifridge?

She hung everything up and reached forward, polished fin-gernails catching on the small fridge clasp. She pulled, easing it open, revealing a row of half-size wine bottles, some im-ported beer, gin, vodka, scotch and some lovely little bottles of champagne.

Oh, she was definitely worth it.

She quickly located a crystal flute in another cabinet, pulled off the foil and wire from the bottle top and popped out the cork. It flew in the air, landing in the steaming tub, making her smile for the first time in an hour.

Raif, she decided firmly, could darn well wait.

She poured herself a tall glass of champagne, set it on the tile shelf and stepped into the tub, moaning softly as she eased her body down into the scented water.

A knock sounded on the door. "Ann?"

"I'm busy."

"What's going on?"

Ann lifted the glass of bubbly champagne and took a sip. Very nice.

"Ann?"

"I'm busy," she repeated, leaning back.

"Doing what?"

"That is a very rude question."

"Were you filling the tub?"

"Are you aware there's a minibar in here?"

Raif was silent for a moment. "I was not."

"I'm drinking champagne. It's pretty good. They'll charge that to the room when you check out, right?" She took another drink.

"I imagine they will."

"Good."

"Bring it out here."

"No."

"Roark called back."

Right. Ann wasn't about to fall for that. "He did not."

"He says he'll bring me the statue."

She took a long drink, settling deeper into the tub, letting the water lap around her neck. "Go away, Raif. You're holding me here, fine. You're keeping me from working, fine. But can we at least be honest with each other?"

"Tomorrow afternoon."

She wished she'd thought to turn off the light. "That's when you're letting me go?"

"That's when we're meeting Roark."

Then she spotted a slider switch on the wall. She stretched up, moving the slider downward. The lights dimmed, then went dark. That was better.

Candlelight flickered against the white-and-gold-tiled wall. The champagne eased its way into her bloodstream. She closed her eyes.

"Ann?"

"I'm ignoring you."

He went silent again, and she listened for retreating footsteps.

But then his gravelly voice came through the door. "You're impossible."

"I'm exhausted." She was, both physically and mentally. It had been a very long five months. She was actually beginning to hope she did get fired. Like tearing off a Band-Aid. At least then it would all be over.

"You have to come out sometime."

She knew she would. But not right now. Right now, for just a little while, she was going to hide away from her problems.

"Ann?" Raif repeated, lowering himself into one of two armchairs decorating the wide hallway outside the master bedroom. His mind conjured up an image of her lounging naked in the big tub, steam wafting over her golden hair, water glistening on her ivory skin.

"Go away," she told him again, voice muffled by the closed door.

He knew he should do just that. But he was intrigued by her. Few men, and no women, challenged him the way she did. Well, maybe Kalila, but only lately, and only since they'd let her spend the school year in Turkey.

"I'm not going away," he told her.

"Are you guarding the door?"

"Something like that."

"You're keeping me from work, Raif. You're probably getting me fired."

"You're keeping me from my family," he countered.

"Am I all that's stopping you? Because, please, by all means, return to your family."

He couldn't help but chuckle at her adroit response. If he set aside the circumstance, he had to admit she was an interesting conversationalist. He cleared his throat and settled into the chair. "What would you be doing?"

"Where?"

"At work. What would you be working on at this time of night?"

"I'm supposed to be at an auction. Antique jewelry, very large pieces, all with an impressive provenance. Most have a European royal connection, but some have links to Hollywood and politics."

"Like Baron Lesley's watch fob?" He gave a random example.

"Or Countess Bayona's emerald necklace. It's the billionaire's version of last-minute Christmas shopping."

Raif stretched out his legs. "I wouldn't mind picking up something for Kalila."

It wouldn't hurt to remind his cousin of the perks of her birthright. Her British college student wouldn't be able to afford antique emeralds.

"You want to go check it out?" asked Ann. "I could get you past security."

Again, Raif chuckled. "Nice try."

"Lot 263 is a very lovely tiara from the court of Louis XVI. I bet it would look great on Kalila. Our estimate is three million. Small change for a guy like you. In fact, I bet you can afford to buy me another bottle of this champagne."

Raif sat up straight. "You drank a whole bottle of champagne?"

"They're teeny, tiny bottles." He heard the water slosh as she moved.

"Ann, I can't let you lie in there and get drunk."

"I don't see how you're going to stop me. The door's locked."

As if a bathroom door lock was going to keep him out. "You'll drown."

"Your concern for my safety is touching. Or is it just that you need me alive long enough to trade me for the statue?"

"I'm not going to harm you."

Though that was more than Raif could say about Ann herself. Too much liquor didn't mix well with hot bathwater.

He heard a popping sound.

"It's Bollinger," Ann announced. "Grande Année. Not something I can normally afford. So, thank you," she rambled on. "Did you know a buyer once paid $275,000 at auction for a bottle of 1907 Heidsieck? It was shipwrecked. So there's that provenance again. But, still, impressive, don't you think?"

"Impressive," Raif agreed. "You'll tell me if you're getting drunk?"

"Oh, I'm definitely getting drunk."

"Am I going to have to come in there and rescue you?"

She laughed. "Wouldn't that be a twist?"

"I'm serious, Ann. I can't have you guzzling champagne and slipping under the water in my hotel room."

"Don't worry, Raif," she sang. "They won't charge you with murder. You have diplomatic immunity."

"Maybe so. But if you stop talking, I'm coming in there."

"I stayed in here for some peace and quiet, not to carry on a conversation with you."

"Tough."

She went silent.

"Ann?"

"I'm still amongst the living."

More silence.

"I can easily pick the lock."

"Fine," she huffed. "What do you want me to talk about?"

"A detailed description of the route to the place where you stashed the *Gold Heart* statue would be nice."

"Let me see... Okay. Here it is. Out the front door of the suite, down the private elevator, through the lobby, take the 60th Street exit to 3rd. Left on 3rd to 37th, through the tunnel to JFK. After that, I'm not so sure."

"Very funny."

"I do have a good sense of humor. Did you know that about me? No. Probably not. Since you're always annoying me." Water sloshed again as she shifted in the tub. "Ever since we met, Raif, you have been a thorn in my side."

"You were a thorn in my side long before we met."

"Yeah, yeah. I know. Because I stole your statue."

"Roark stole it. But you're the one fencing it."

"You do know there's a great, big, wide hole in your theory."

"Do tell."

"Waverly's can't deal in stolen property. We'd lose our license, be brought up on charges, devalue the company, get taken over by Rothschild's. Why, oh, why do you imagine we'd be so foolish?"

"You didn't think you'd get caught."

"We *advertised*."

"In English. In Western publications."

"On the internet."

"You likely assumed Rayas didn't have the internet." He gave a silent shrug. "Or maybe you did believe Roark Black. At first. But you should have rectified the mistake as soon as it was brought to your attention."

It took her a moment to answer. "So should you. It's a co-incidence, nothing more."

"I don't believe in coincidences." Raif couldn't get past the astronomical odds that his statue had been stolen at the exact same time as the one that had supposedly gone down with the *Titanic* mysteriously surfaced. It defied logic and reason.

"Ann?"

She didn't answer.

Raif came to his feet. "Ann?"

He rattled the doorknob.

Still no answer.

Reaching into the pocket of his slacks, he retrieved a folding multipurpose tool from his pocket, slipping open the narrow pick.

"I'm fine," came Ann's voice.

Then the door opened, and she stood in the door frame, wrapped in a huge white robe, her hair damp and her skin glowing.

"No need to panic," she told him.

Raif gritted his teeth and held his tongue. Half of him wanted to shake her senseless, the other half wanted to pull her into his arms and bury his face in her lavender-scented skin.

She pulled the lapels together, hiding her delicate neck. "I'm hungry," she announced. "I was going to stand on principle and refuse to accept anything from you. But I've changed my mind. Order me something expensive, Kobe beef or Scottish lobster. Maybe some quail's eggs or white truffles."

"Is this your little rebellion?"

"Yes." Her lips pursed in a pout, and he desperately wanted to kiss it away.

He resisted. "You do know you can't bankrupt me by eating."

"Then order me up a side of red diamonds."

"Two million a carat. Nice choice."

"How do you know their value so precisely?"

"Queen Elizabeth presented one to my mother from the Argyle mines in Australia."

"You've met Queen Elizabeth?"

"Yes."

"The queen of England."

"The very same. I went to school for two years at Oxford."

"So did thousands of other people. They didn't meet the queen."

"The red diamond was before I went to Oxford. The queen

was greeting the Rayasian royal party in Sydney, mostly because a number of Commonwealth nations want to trade for our lanthanum."

"And how much lanthanum does one get in exchange for a red diamond?"

Raif found himself smiling. "It's not quid pro quo. There weren't gentlemen standing there with scales or anything."

"So, your mother gets a red diamond simply to give Commonwealth countries the opportunity to make a deal with Rayas for lanthanum."

"That about covers it."

She tipped her head sideways. "Is there anything in life you can't have, Raif Khouri?"

You.

He gave himself a mental shake. But still, the air seemed to thicken between them.

Her gaze softened on his. Her pink cheeks seemed to go a shade darker. Then her red lips parted ever so slightly.

Of its own accord, his hand moved to the lapel on her robe, his skin dark against the stark white of the thick fabric. He fisted around it, eased her closer, his head dipping down, canting sideway, fitting his lips over the softness of hers.

She gave a soft exclamation, before their kiss blocked out the sound. Her taste rocked through him, sweetened by the champagne, just like he remembered. She didn't resist, her lips parted, giving him access, letting him into the deeper, sweeter recesses of her mouth.

His free hand wrapped around her waist, pulling her close, holding her soft, warm body tight against his own. He'd missed this. He'd dreamed of this. He'd longed for the feel of her in his arms every damn night since they'd kissed in Rayas.

But then she pushed against his shoulders, dragging her mouth from his. "Raif, no."

Yes! "Nobody's here. No one can get a picture." There was a fire in his belly, and it couldn't be extinguished by her protest.

"That's not the point."

"What is the point?" He reluctantly removed his hand from her waist, resting it against the doorjamb, partially trapping her in place.

"We're fighting."

"So what?"

"I'm your captive."

"That just makes it sexier."

She smacked the heel of her hand against his shoulder. "This isn't Rayas."

He couldn't seem to stop the half smile that formed on his face. "If this was Rayas, you'd already be in my bed." In fact, she'd have been in his bed days ago, right after the charity party.

"Am I supposed to be grateful for your restraint?"

For a moment, he allowed himself to be honest. He let go of her lapel and brushed his fingers beneath her chin. "Yes, you are. Because, Ann Richardson, I am showing restraint. You are the most enchanting, exciting, amazingly beautiful woman I have ever met."

"Very funny."

"Maybe it's because you rebuff me," he mused. "Or maybe there really is a curse to the statue, but I want you very, very badly."

"I was told that you don't believe in the curse."

"I don't," he concurred. "But all I can think about is you, watching you."

"Quit joking around, Raif."

"I'm not joking around."

"You don't like me."

"And you don't like me. But we both know you'll kiss me back. You're cursed, too, Ann."

She opened her mouth, but seemed to decide against speaking.

"We'll order something to eat," he told her, determined to let his morals and principles win this one. "Something ridiculously expensive if that's what you want. But for the rest of tonight, you are going to burn in my brain. I'm going to want you every second we're together."

Silence fell between them, and Ann's chest rose and fell with what looked like very deep breaths. Her color was high, and her blue eyes sparkled like sapphires.

When she finally spoke, her voice was throaty, barely above a whisper. "It's a good thing you have diplomatic immunity. Because I'm pretty sure what you just said was illegal."

Raif forced himself to straighten away from her, dropping his arm and putting some space between them. "Everything's illegal in America. It's a wonder anyone here stays out of jail."

"It's a wonder that the women of your country haven't killed you while you slept."

He grinned and shook his head. "You've got spunk, Ann. Too bad it's not coupled with honesty."

For the first time since he'd met her, she seemed to drop her guard. Her blue eyes turned clear and direct, level and intelligent. "Let me be honest. I would kiss you back. But that doesn't make it okay. We might be attracted to each other on some kind of chemical level, but you and me is a very, very bad idea."

Intellectually, he agreed with her. But there were other forces at work here, powerful forces, inexorable forces. He hated to admit it to himself, but he was beginning to seriously consider the possibility of the *Gold Heart* curse. He knew Ann was the worst choice in the world for him. And he was normally a disciplined man. But he couldn't seem to stop himself from wanting her.

Four

Against all earthly odds, the next afternoon, Ann found herself staring at Roark Black across a cold, stark, abandoned warehouse. Raif had brought her to an industrial area on the waterfront in Queens. He was now beside and slightly behind her as they faced Roark from about thirty feet away. Raif's hand was clamped firmly around her upper arm, holding her when she would have gone to Roark.

Both men had driven their vehicles into the building. Raif's a dark gray Mercedes, and Roark's a black SUV. Roark set a thick envelope down on a small, dusty bench between them.

"Back away," Raif ordered.

Roark held up his palms and took a few steps back.

As Raif urged her forward, Ann found her voice.

"Roark, what are you—"

"Quiet," Raif demanded.

"But—"

"Shut up," he growled in her ear.

Ann closed her mouth. There'd be time enough later to ask Roark why he'd taken the risk of meeting them.

Raif stopped her at the table and dumped the contents of the envelope.

"A letter from Princess Salima," said Roark. "Gifting her *Gold Heart* statue to a prison guard named Zaruri at Traitor's Prison. It seems Zaruri sprung Salima's lover, Cosmo, and the two ran away together, boarding the *Titanic* to be married."

As Roark spoke, Ann found herself drawn into the story.

"Zaruri secretly sold the statue in Dubai," Roark continued. "I'm assuming he was afraid of your ancestors' wrath. I've pieced together chain of title up to and including Waverly's right to sell it at auction. The documentation was stolen there for a while. But I have it all back."

Raif gave a cursory glance at each of the documents. "Where's my statue?"

"This is all you need," Roark countered. "And it's not your statue."

Raif waved a dismissive hand over the pile of papers. "Nice story, but these are easy enough to forge."

"Easy enough to validate, too."

"Not in the next five minutes." Raif's tone turned guttural. "Where's the statue? I keep Ann until I see it for myself."

"I don't think so." There was a menacing thread to Roark's tone, and Ann glanced up to see him advancing on them, fists clenched by his side.

Her heart stood still.

"Let her go," Roark ordered.

But Raif pushed Ann behind him, squaring his shoulders, clearly ready to fight. "You don't want to do this. Nobody wins. Bring me the statue and you can have her back."

Roark seemed to hesitate "It's not here."

"Where is it?"

Roark didn't say a word.

Raif began to back away, urging Ann toward the vehicle. "Get it. Name a time and place, and I'll meet you again."

Roark's dark gaze pinned Ann. She could feel his frustration and his uncertainty.

"Don't do anything," she told him in a choked voice, afraid a fight would end up with someone seriously injured. "I'll be fine."

She didn't exactly fear for her life, nor for her physical safety. For some reason, she believed Raif wouldn't harm her.

"Please," she asked him. "Just get the statue. I'll be fine. We'll meet you somewhere."

"You son of a bitch," Roark growled.

"Bring me the statue," Raif repeated. "And this will all be over."

"Here," said Roark, tone bitter. "Tomorrow night, eight o'clock."

Ann wished she could say something more to reassure him. She should be able to find a way to make the situation better. But her throat was chalk-dry, and her brain felt as though it was moving through molasses.

Raif gave a brisk nod and waited while Roark retrieved the paperwork, climbed into his SUV and peeled out of the building.

Then Raif let go of Ann. "*What* is the *matter* with you people?"

She rounded on him. "With us? With *us*?"

"My instructions were simple. Bring me the statue. How hard is that?" Raif breathed deeply, slowing his voice down, enunciating each word. "Bring me the statue."

"He brought you the proof," Ann countered. As far as she was concerned, the chain of title was more important than the statue itself. The three were nearly identical. Documented provenance was the only way to verify which statue was in Roark's possession.

"Any kid with a printer in his basement could mock up those documents."

"Those are the originals. You can date the ink. You can date the paper. Surely, you can verify Princess Salima's signature."

"Not here I can't."

Ann shook her head, giving up. Arguing with Raif was like

arguing with a brick wall. Once he got an idea locked up there in his brain, dynamite wouldn't blast it out.

"What now?" she asked him.

He moved to open the passenger door for her. "Well, we're sure not going back to the Plaza. Too many people might have seen us leave there. And who knows what Roark will say to the police."

"You mean he might tell them the truth?" She got into the car. She might not know Raif's plans for her, but staying here in this dank, cold building wasn't going to help anything.

"Exactly." He slammed the door behind her.

Ann dropped her head back on the leather headrest.

"What if he shows up tomorrow with the SWAT team?" she asked as Raif slid into the driver's seat.

He adjusted the rearview mirror. "Then I guess I get arrested."

"What kind of a plan is that?" she demanded.

"I'm playing the odds. If he's got a stolen statue, he doesn't want the police here any more than we do."

"We?"

Raif frowned at her. "If, by some miracle, he has Princess Salima's statue, then he wants to prove that to me and quietly get you back." Raif started the engine, pulling the car into a tight circle. "Roark works in the shadows, Ann. He gets things done quietly and cleanly. The last thing he wants is a circus."

"You've got a lot riding on that," she observed. Although she privately understood Raif's logic, odds aside, he had no idea what Roark might or might not do.

"I've had a lot riding on this since my *Gold Heart* was stolen. I have a seriously ill father, craving peace of mind. I have a sister about to run off with a Brit and sour Rayas's relationship with a key ally, causing anything from protests in the street, to a trade war, to an actual war. And I have a country who will need to have faith in my leadership. How can they have faith in my leadership if I lose a vital national artifact and curse the royal family?"

"I thought you didn't believe in the curse," Ann couldn't help but note.

"I don't. But others do. Kalila shirks her royal duty, and Rayasians blame the *Gold Heart* curse."

"And you're the guy who can't find the statue," Ann observed quietly. For the first time, she thought she understood Raif's single-minded determination to find it.

"I'm the guy who can't find the statue."

"I wish I could help you," she told him honestly. She still had complete confidence in Roark, and that meant something else had happened to Raif's statue. He deserved to get it back.

"Right," he scoffed. "You've been nothing but helpful through all of this."

As they drove down a gravel-strewn, potholed street on the East River, Ann turned sideways in her seat. "Think about it, Raif. What if I'm not lying? What if Roark's not lying? What if this is a bizarre coincidence, and someone else stole your statue?"

"I don't believe in coincidences."

"Play along with me," she cajoled. After all, they had nothing better to do for the next twenty-four hours.

"That the two events are completely independent?"

"Yes. Who would steal your statue?"

"Somebody who wanted to sell it."

"Or somebody who wanted to mess with your family. You just said it would impact your credibility. Your father is sick, and your people need to have faith." For some reason, the magnitude of that particular revelation overcame her. Her shoulders dropped. "You're going to be the king," she found herself stating in wonder.

"And?" he prompted.

"And, how can you wrap your head around that?"

The industrial buildings and junkyards turned to retail space and apartment buildings. The road beneath them smoothed out, and traffic lights appeared, along with pedestrians and taxicabs.

"I've known it was coming for a while now," said Raif.

It was hard to believe she was sitting with a future monarch. She found herself suddenly curious. "How does it work, exactly? Being king? Do you sit around on a throne all day, crown on your head, while people come before you and ask for things?"

Raif laughed, and the rich sound of it seemed to permeate Ann's body. She found herself relaxing, her worries tamping down, her fear going away.

"Something like that," he told her. "I'll mostly have to shake hands, exchange pleasantries and gifts, and sit in interminable meetings where government officials enlighten me on their pet projects and ask for money from the treasury."

"So, you're in charge of the money?"

"I have accountants who help me."

"But the money, for an entire country, is under your control?"

"Ultimately, yes."

She pondered that. "How many people are in Rayas?"

"Ten million, give or take."

"And what do they do?"

"You mean besides bow and scrape to their king?"

"Besides that."

"Mining, of course, the rare earths, tourism, some agriculture," he rattled off. "We have an up-and-coming wine industry. We also have a major port, so shipping. Our financial sector is not as strong as Dubai, but a close second for the region. The southern city of Tarku has a world-class university with both high-technology and medical-research facilities. We see that as a key segment of the national economy going forward."

Ann was momentarily stunned to silence. "Seriously?"

"What part?"

"The whole thing. A port, a financial center, high-tech. Most of the buildings in the capital looked historic. And I thought it was the only significant city."

"You were picturing nomads and camel races in the countryside?"

"Well…"

"It's possible to have a traditional social structure and a modern economy."

"It's not common."

"It's more common than you think. Though, I do admit, it is a point of pride for my father that his country be the best of both worlds." Raif slowed for a traffic light.

Ann couldn't resist. "How is it the best of both worlds for women?"

He gave her a sideways glance but didn't answer.

"Those women who have no choice but to sleep with you?" she pressed. "How is it good for them?"

"I don't force women to sleep with me."

"Of course not. All those concubines are 'willing.' Come on, Raif. They know they can't refuse."

He gave a low chuckle. "I don't know what you're picturing, Ann. Or maybe I do know what you're picturing. But let me assure you, I don't have concubines. I go on dates. Just like you. I'm sometimes introduced to a woman who is interested in me, and who I find interesting, and we spend time together."

"And sleep together."

It was obvious he was making it sound more civilized than it was.

He pulled through the intersection with the rest of the traffic. "You don't sleep with your dates?"

"Not with all of them," she huffed. "And certainly not on the first date."

"But you've had relationships?"

"I'm not a virgin, if that's what you're asking."

"Neither am I."

Ann rolled her eyes. "No kidding."

"I'm saying it's the same thing in Rayas as it is in America. People go out on dates. Some engage in physical intimacy, and some do not."

"And there's no social stigma?" she pressed, not believing he was giving an accurate picture.

It seemed as though a left turn suddenly needed his complete concentration.

"Raif?" she prompted.

"Hmm?"

"Would you marry a woman who wasn't a virgin?"

"No."

"But there's no social stigma," she mocked.

"The future queen would be expected to maintain a certain standard of behavior."

"But, not the future king."

Raif obviously fought a smirk. "The future king is discreet."

"I pity the future queen."

"Hey, she'll have palaces, jewels, servants and me. I would think saving her virginity would be a small price to pay."

"You have someone in mind?" Ann couldn't help asking.

He shook his head. "Not so far."

"I was just thinking, you might want to cloister her soon. You know, just to be safe."

"Maybe I should cloister a dozen or so, that way I'll have my pick."

Ann pretended to contemplate the idea. "You don't want to let them out of their houses, or their palaces, I guess. So, do you have to marry someone royal?"

"It's preferable."

"I suppose it's easier to safeguard the chastity of someone with security around her."

"You seem to have an obsession about this," Raif observed.

"I think it's a double standard."

"I'm not saying unmarried women can't have a sex life."

"You're only saying you won't marry one who does."

He pinned her with a sharp gaze. "That's because I will be king."

"If you weren't going to be king?"

The intensity of his stare seemed to grow. "I'd marry whoever I wanted."

"Virgin or not?"

"Virgin or not, royalty or not, Rayasian or not. But I have my duty, Ann."

"What about Kalila?"

"She has her duty, too."

"Do you think she's a virgin?"

"If she's not, then that Brit better never set foot on Rayasian soil."

Ann couldn't help but smile. "You are such a hypocrite."

"I am not."

"Would you sleep with me?"

Raif twisted his head to stare at her, his gaze sending a wave of awareness through her body. "In a heartbeat."

"But you wouldn't respect me in the morning?" she asked, instantly realizing the question had been a mistake and struggling to hold on to the through-thread of her argument.

"Why would you care?"

She caught a flash of red in the corner of her eye. "Raif, look out!"

His attention shot back to the windshield, and he swerved to narrowly miss a red Corvette, then he quickly twisted the wheel to pull the Mercedes out of the path of oncoming traffic.

Fear had jolted her, but arousal had heightened her senses. If Raif looked at her like that again, she might just throw herself into his arms. She had no problem believing the women he had slept with in the past were perfectly willing.

"Where are we going?" she asked, deciding she'd better change the subject.

"Long Island."

"What's in Long Island?"

"My cousin Tariq."

"Your cousin lives on Long Island?"

"It's a rental— Damn."

As Raif swore, Ann heard the blast of a siren and caught the flash of blue-and-red lights behind them.

Her reflexive reaction of alarm at the prospect of a traffic ticket was quickly quashed by the realization that she was saved. One word from her to the officer, and Raif would be hauled off to jail. Sure, they'd work out the diplomatic immunity thing soon enough. But she'd be free, and safe, and Roark wouldn't have to risk bringing the *Gold Heart* to a clandestine meeting in Queens.

He pulled to the curb, and the squad car swerved in behind.

Raif gripped the steering wheel, staring straight ahead for a very long moment. Then he turned to look at her, his expression a study in stoic resignation. She had to hand it to him. He was taking this like a man. Then she had to work very hard not to grin.

Take that, Raif Khouri.

A brawny uniformed officer tapped on Raif's window.

Raif pushed a button on the door handle, and the window slid smoothly down.

"Afternoon, sir," said the officer.

"Afternoon," Raif responded.

"You swerved into oncoming traffic back there."

"It was an evasive maneuver, around the red Corvette."

"Didn't see a red Corvette."

Raif didn't respond.

"Can I see your driver's license?"

Raif reached into his breast pocket, extracting his wallet and producing the license.

The officer read for a moment. "I see you're not licensed to drive in the state of New York."

Raif turned in his seat to fully face the officer. "It's an international driver's license." Then he handed over his passport.

A few more moments passed.

"Rayas?" asked the officer.

"Yes."

"That in Africa?"

"Near Dubai."

The officer backed off a pace. "Can you step out of the car, please?"

"Of course." Raif glanced once more at Ann, searching her expression. Then he gave her a brief nod of acquiescence. "Goodbye, Ann."

"Goodbye, Raif."

A sharp rap on the window behind her made Ann jump. She turned to see another officer outside the car. Her chest tightened. This was it. She was going to start talking, and Raif would be slapped in handcuffs.

Probably the first time that had ever happened.

It took her a minute to find the right button, but then she smoothly rolled down the window.

"Ma'am," the officer said in greeting. He was maybe six feet tall, slim, but with broad shoulders, a hat perched on what looked like a shaved head. His utility belt looked like it weighed about twenty pounds.

"Hello, officer," Ann responded.

"Are you from Rayas, too?"

Ann shook her head, wondering how to broach the subject of her kidnapping. Did she blurt it right out? Did she wait for the right question, the right opening?

"This man a friend of yours?"

She shook her head again.

Say it. Say it, a voice demanded inside her head.

"We have mutual business interests" was what came out.

The officer's expression turned suspicious. "And what might those mutual business interests be?"

"Auctions," said Ann, swallowing. What was she doing? Why didn't she turn Raif in?

For some reason, his words about Roark wanting to keep things clean and quiet rang in her ears. Would Roark prefer to handle this without the police? Did she trust that Roark had the legitimate statue? She'd have sworn on a stack of bibles that she trusted him.

Her entire body turned hot, then cold, then hot again. "I work for an auction house, and Prince Raif has—"

"*Prince* Raif?"

"Yes."

"Hey, Amseth," the officer called to his partner. "I hear you've got a prince over there."

Ann couldn't hear the partner's answer.

Then the officer turned back to Ann. "Can I see some identification?"

She hesitated for a split second. Had someone reported her missing by now? Had Darby grown worried, or had someone at Waverly's realized she was gone?

But she had no choice, so she extracted her wallet and handed the officer her driver's license.

"Wait here, ma'am," he said, turning to walk away.

She glanced over her left shoulder, seeing Raif still standing with the first officer. They were too tall for her to see their faces, so she had no idea what was happening.

The traffic whirred by, people craning their necks to see what was going on. She felt like a criminal. Which wasn't fair. It wasn't fair at all.

The officer reappeared, handing her back her license. "Thank you, Ms. Richardson."

"You're welcome," she offered automatically, taking back the license.

She slipped it back in her wallet, her mind at war with itself. This was her last chance. She could speak up now, or remain at Raif's mercy. Was she stupid? Was she crazy? Was she deluding herself in thinking Raif was a fair and reasonable man?

Just because he seemed to care about his family, and just because his father was sick, and just because he was sexy and funny and he'd behaved like a gentleman despite having diplomatic immunity and despite her enthusiastic kisses last night.

"Have a good day, ma'am," the officer finished, turning away. And just like that, her chance was gone.

A few seconds later, Raif stepped into the driver's seat.

He slammed the door. His jaw was set. He started the engine, glanced in the mirror and pulled back into traffic.

They were both silent for about two blocks.

"For future reference," he ground out, sounding unaccountably angry, "if anything like this ever happens to you again, you *tell* the cops you're being kidnapped." He slammed the heels of his hands down on the steering wheel. "What the hell is the matter with you, Ann Richardson?"

"I don't know," she admitted in a small voice.

"Why didn't you give me up?" he demanded.

She shot Raif a furtive glance. "I'm not sure. You didn't take advantage of me last night. And I guess I decided to trust in Roark."

Raif turned to stare at her.

"Watch the road," she reminded him.

He turned his attention back to the traffic, pushing hard on the brake as they came to a red light. "You're not making sense."

"You said Roark would want to take care of this discreetly." She struggled to sound certain about her decision. "I know he has the legitimate statue, and I'm going to let him handle it his way. If he wants to call the cops, he'll call the cops."

Raif seemed unsure of how to respond.

The walls of Raif's cousin's rental house were made almost entirely of glass. The house was an offset V shape, set on a rocky bluff, with a great room that angled away from the entrance hall. The great room was rectangular in shape, overlooking the ocean on one side and the pool deck on the other. The pool was empty, the deck furniture draped in weatherproof covers and sprinkled with a skiff of snow.

Raif shut the door behind Ann, watching as her gaze took in the cream-colored sofa grouping and the polished maple tables. Through the glass beyond her, the ocean was restless, breakers coming in on the rocks below, while freighters, barges and the occasional yacht cut the water out in the channel. The sun was setting behind the Manhattan skyline, barely shining through the gray winter clouds.

"What happened?" asked Tariq, as he moved through the kitchen. "And what's she doing here?" Tariq's gaze went from Ann to Raif and back again.

"Change of plans," said Raif. "Roark met up with us, but he didn't bring the statue."

"That doesn't explain what she's doing here," said Tariq.

"He kidnapped me," Ann offered.

Raif couldn't exactly deny it.

"*That* was your plan?" Tariq demanded in disbelief. "To ransom Ann Richardson?"

"I tried to keep you out of it," said Raif.

"Have you been with him since last night?" Tariq asked Ann.

"All night long," she responded. "He kept me locked in the penthouse, under guard, stole my cell phone, disconnected the others."

"Are you unfamiliar with the laws of the United States?" Tariq asked Raif. "Because, I can enlighten you. I had to memorize them in order to pass the bar."

"He has diplomatic immunity," Ann pointed out.

"That doesn't excuse kidnapping." Though Tariq was speaking to Ann, his rebuke was obviously for Raif.

"She's here willingly…now," said Raif.

"That's a stretch," Ann noted.

Tariq moved to a wall and flicked on the lights. They glowed soft yellow in the gathering gloom, rebounding against the wooden floor and the high-beamed ceiling.

"So, what's your new plan?" he asked. "Do I need to call in a chopper so we can make a run for Teterboro?"

"Roark says he'll bring me the statue tomorrow."

"And you believe him this time?"

Raif flicked a glance to Ann, silhouetted against the darkening glass. "I believe he wants Ann back. And I know it's not in his best interests to involve the police."

Ann's faith in Roark was misplaced. But Raif was counting on Roark understanding that he was trapped. There was no way out, except to give up the statue.

"If he calls the police, they'll deport you," Tariq warned.

"They'll let me back in," Raif countered.

"Maybe you. But they'll kick me out for good, and then they'll disbar me."

Ann looked to Tariq. "You're licensed to practice law in America?"

"I'm a Harvard graduate."

"And you couldn't talk some sense into this guy?"

Tariq cracked a smile. "Nobody can talk any sense into this guy."

She nodded in obvious sympathy. "Lord knows I've tried."

"You two do remember I'm still here," Raif drawled.

"You're the cause of all this," said Ann.

"*You're* the cause of all this," he retorted.

She half turned to face him, crossing her arms over her chest. "I was minding my own business, doing my job, living my regularly scheduled life."

"What do you think I was doing?"

"There's nothing regular about your life."

Tariq chuckled.

"You forget yourself," Raif barked.

"Apologies, Your Royal Highness."

It was Ann's turn to glance from one man to the other. "You're kidding, right?" Her gaze did another sweep. "You actually call him that?"

"Absolutely," Tariq confirmed.

"It's my title," Raif huffed.

"Not in my book."

"In Rayas," Tariq said softly, "his subjects bow in his presence and wait to be spoken to."

"That's ridiculous," said Ann.

Tariq shook his head. "It's protocol."

Her eyes narrowed in Raif's direction. "I guess I've been breaking protocol."

"Let me count the ways."

If they were in Rayas, he'd have had no choice but to punish her. While he was a good deal less formal than his father, theirs was an absolute monarchy, and deference to the royal hierarchy was vital to the good order of the country.

She gave a shallow curtsy. "Allow me to apologize, Your Royal Highness."

"Mocking doesn't count," he pointed out.

She grinned. "I don't seem to be able to do this seriously."

"I was thinking about ordering pizza," said Tariq.

"Works for me," Raif acknowledged. He was starving. "Any beer in the fridge?"

"I'll grab you one." Tariq made for the kitchen.

"This is surreal," said Ann.

Raif gave a shrug. "We'll need our strength tomorrow."

Five

Barefoot, clad in her ivory slip, Ann padded past the empty pizza box on the dining room table several hours later. Lying in bed at about 2:00 a.m., she'd suddenly realized the rented house probably had landline phones. She hadn't found one in her bedroom, nor in the big living room. But, in the kitchen, she'd hit the jackpot.

Standing on the cool terra-cotta tiles, she removed the cordless phone from its cradle. She dialed her home voice mail number and listened in relief while the signal rang through. She entered her code, but found that she didn't have any messages. That was odd. She'd at least expected someone from work to have checked on her. Next, she tried Darby's number.

It was dark inside the house, but the glow of Manhattan filtered across the water and through the glass wall. Ann imagined Darby in her apartment, waking from sleep, shaking her head, glancing at her clock and then blindly reaching for her phone.

"Hello?" came her sleep-husky voice.

"Darby? It's Ann."

"Huh? What? Ann?"

Now Ann could picture Darby shaking her wits back into her head, raking back her messy hair, sitting in her bed.

"Where are you?" Darby asked.

"I'm in Long Island."

"Long Island? Why? What are you doing there? Are you okay?"

"I'm okay," Ann assured her. "It's a long story. But has anyone missed me?"

"Have you been gone?"

"Just overnight."

"Oh. Sorry. I didn't notice. But I would have missed you if I'd known."

"What about anyone at Waverly's? Edwina? Did they ask about me?"

"Nobody's called me. And I haven't seen Edwina. Why? Are you actually missing?"

"I haven't been home since Friday."

"Oh, you're *with a man?*"

"No, I'm not *with a man.*"

Well, okay, Ann was with a man. But not the way Darby meant.

"I didn't go to the auction Friday night," Ann explained.

"You skipped work?"

"I did." Now that Ann thought about it, she supposed it was possible nobody had noticed she was gone. She was always in and out, back and forth between the main and smaller auction rooms, helping with the merchandise as well as in the back office with the paperwork. It was a little unsettling, but entirely possible that everyone simply assumed she was somewhere else.

She heard a rustling in the background at Darby's end of the phone.

"All right," said Darby. "I'm comfortable now. Go ahead."

"Roark surfaced."

"That's great."

"It's complicated. I really just wanted to let you know I was okay." Though it sounded as though she needn't have bothered. Nobody seemed to have noticed she was gone, never mind raised an alarm. "I can't talk long."

"Oh, no, you don't. It's after two, and I'm wide-awake now."

That was a fair point. Ann glanced around the big, dark kitchen and listened to the quiet of the house. What did it matter if she lost a little sleep?

"I'm with Raif," she told Darby.

"The prince?"

"Yes."

"You're spending the weekend with the Neanderthal who thinks you stole his statue?"

"I'm not 'spending the weekend' with him."

"You said you hadn't been home since Friday."

Another fair point. Why did Darby's mind have to be so sharp in the middle of the night?

"Okay, I guess I am spending the weekend with him. But not in bed."

"You sure?"

"Yes, I'm sure. I can tell whether or not there's a man in my bed."

Not that she hadn't thought about it. This particular man was one heck of a kisser. And, once you got past the arrogance and the felonies, he was an awfully sexy guy. He even had a decent sense of humor. And he was certainly entertaining in an argument.

"Ann?"

"What?"

"You went silent there for a minute."

"Oh, sorry."

"Were you picturing him naked?"

Ann felt her face heat. Thank goodness Darby wasn't in the same room. "No, I was *not* picturing him naked."

"Have you seen him naked?"

"Is this really what you want to talk about?"

"Sure."

Ann cracked a smile at that. "Fine. Let me be clear. Despite what the tabloids might decide to say, I'm not off on a clandestine affair. The man kidnapped me."

"Wait a minute. Back up. Are you in danger?"

"No."

"Are you sure? Man, we should have a code word or something."

"I'm sure. It's going to be fine. He's ransoming me to Roark for the statue."

"You want me to call the cops?" asked Darby.

Ann braced her hand against the cool glass, Manhattan blurring in her vision. "No. I think it's better for everyone if I see this through."

"You *think?*"

"Okay, I know it's better for everyone. And it's going to be fine. Roark says he has the statue. Once Raif knows it's legitimate, he'll go home, and this will all be over. Honestly, if Raif wanted to do me harm, he had his chance last night."

There was a lilt of excitement in Darby's tone. "Did he blindfold you? Toss you in the trunk? Tie you to a chair? No, wait, the bed. Did he tie you to his bed?"

"He did not tie me to his bed." Ann dropped her hand and turned from the window. "Not that he didn't—" She caught Raif's laconic pose, leaning against the kitchen doorjamb, arms folded across his bare chest, gray sweatpants riding low on his hips, one ankle crossed over the other.

"—uh, behave like a jerk," she said into the phone.

Raif raised his brows.

"Gotta go," she said to Darby.

"But this is just getting good," Darby protested.

"I'll call you tomorrow. I'm fine. Don't worry."

"Who's worried? I'm curious."

"Bye," Ann repeated, pressing the disconnect button before Darby had a chance to say anything else.

Then she deliberately set down the phone and glared at Raif. "How long have you been eavesdropping?"

"Long enough," he answered easily.

Her mind scrambled to remember the details of the conversation. What had she given away?

"Long enough for what?" she demanded.

"Long enough to know you're not picturing me naked."

She fought a rise of heat in her cheeks. "I'm definitely not," she informed him tartly.

"So you said."

"Yes, I did." She had said that, and it proved that Raif naked was the farthest thing from her mind.

His slow gaze moved from her tousled hair, to her bare shoulders, over her thinly veiled breasts, to the lace hem of her satin slip, all the way to her toes. Her skin tingled in his wake.

His lazy, brown eyes met hers. "Wish I could say the same thing."

It took a split second for his words to sink in. When it did, a wash of desire bathed her skin. She wouldn't acknowledge it. She didn't dare acknowledge it.

Rattled, she blurted out the first thing that popped into her mind. "Shouldn't you be asleep?"

"I heard you up."

"And?"

"I thought you were probably calling a cab."

"I wasn't."

"So I discovered."

He straightened away from the doorway, moving slowly toward her, watching, like a sleek, bronzed predator. Her heart thudded hard against her chest wall.

"You realize, you did it again," he chided.

She swallowed, gaze glued to his movements. "Did what?"

"You had a chance to save yourself, and you gave it up." He moved inexorably closer.

This time, the heat gathered between her legs. "I'm trusting Roark."

"Are you trusting me?"

"No."

"Are you scared of me?"

"No." Unsettled? Yes. Aroused? Definitely. Frightened? For some reason, she wasn't.

He stopped in front of her. "You should be."

She tipped her head to look up at him, giving her short hair a toss. "Because of your infamous diplomatic immunity and how you might use it against me?"

"In part."

"What's the other part?"

"That I'm going to kiss you." His gaze turned molten. "And that you're going to like it."

"I won't," she denied, swallowing, battling the memory of their last kiss, and the kiss before that. She could smell roses in the palace garden, feel Raif's whiskered chin, taste his hot mouth.

"You already are."

She mutely shook her head, not trusting her own voice.

His lips curved in a knowing smile. "Your lips are soft."

"I'm sleepy," she rasped.

"Your pupils are dilated."

"It's dark."

"Your nipples are hard."

She refused to glance down. "I'm cold."

He eased in. "I like you cold. And I like you sleepy. And I like you in the dark."

Oh, no. "Raif—"

He placed his index finger across her lips. The touch was electric. It sent an instant jolt of desire to the far reaches of her body, and the air involuntarily sucked deep into her lungs.

He moved his finger across her cheek, then cupped her face with his palm. She knew she should bat him away, tell him to stop, pull back and flee to her bedroom. But she was frozen in place.

"I'm not going to tie you to the bed," he whispered, leaning in.

She couldn't think of a single response to his words. She battled her own reaction, searched her brain for a way to dampen her passion. Succumbing to Raif was a colossally bad idea.

"But our situation has changed. You can stay, go or tell me to get lost. You're no longer my captive. I'm holding nothing over you. By this time tomorrow, I'll be back on my Gulfstream, statue in hand, and—"

"They'll hold it for evidence," she blurted out.

He drew back. "What did you say?"

"They'll hold it for evidence. The statue. They won't let you take it with you." She didn't know why she'd said it.

Raif pounced. "So, you admit it was stolen?"

Her brain stumbled for a moment. "I guess I'm considering a long-shot scenario. Like I sometimes worry about falling off tall buildings and being hit by lightning.... More so when I'm with you, it seems."

He shook his head at her meandering argument. But his eyes darkened as his fingers splayed into her hair. The pressure of his palm urged her closer.

"I've just been hit by lightning."

She didn't resist, and his lips dipped down to meet hers.

Every time Raif kissed Ann, it was a fight to keep from tearing off her clothes. The taste of her lips and the scent of her skin hijacked his logic and tore away his grasp on reason. That he wanted to bury himself inside her was the single, primitive thought that pulsed through his brain.

He tried to take it slow, to pay attention to her reaction, her cues. Her assertion that lovers who were also his subjects, or possibly in awe of his royal title, would have faked passion had him questioning himself. Had he become complacent? He didn't want to make any mistakes with Ann.

For now, to his infinite relief, she was wholeheartedly kissing him back. Her lips were soft and sweet beneath his own. They parted, and her small tongue darted into his mouth. Her body molded against his, her soft breasts pressing through the thin satin of her slip to warm his bare skin.

His arms tightened around her narrow waist, palms sliding along her rib cage, then down to her pert bottom, her shapely thighs. The wispy fabric slipped through his fingertips, setting off lightning charges inside his brain. He kissed her harder, deeper, quickly losing his battle with control. He wedged one thigh between her legs, letting his hands cup the curve of her bottom, moving lower to the hem of her slip and finally caressing the warmth of her bare thighs.

He moaned her name, and her arms twined around his neck. Her fingers teased his short hair, swirling along his neckline, shooting pulses of desire down the length of his body.

He scooped her into his arms, breaking their kiss long enough to gaze into her deep blue eyes. He didn't know what he was looking for, but he didn't find it. Her dark lashes swept down and camouflaged her mood. But then they opened again, and she gazed up at him. Passion seemed to simmer in their depths.

But he wasn't making any assumptions. "Are you saying yes?"

She hesitated and for a moment he cursed himself for asking. But then her voice turned as sultry as a desert night. "Yes," she answered.

He turned abruptly for his bedroom, one arm cradling the crook of her bare knees. The other supported her shoulders, his palm wrapped solidly around her rib cage, resting beneath her breast.

In a few long strides he was through the bedroom door. He kicked it shut behind them, locking out the world. He set her on her feet next to the four-poster bed, his arms still around her, glued to hers. Light from the garden filtered through the sheer curtains. The moon was high in the clearing sky, and the stars were muted behind it.

He stroked his thumb across her chin, her cheek, her lips, marveling at her delicate skin, the silk of her hair, the incredible clarity of her eyes.

"You're beautiful," he whispered in awe. The longer he knew her, the more beautiful she became. It was uncanny.

"So are you."

He couldn't help but chuckle at the absurdity of her assertion. But then he fell silent as her hand moved tentatively to his bare chest, small fingers tracing a pattern.

All coherent thought left his brain. There was no today, no tomorrow and certainly no yesterday when he and Ann had been at odds. He closed his eyes to savor her light touch. Flashes of energy seemed to trail behind it. He'd never felt anything like it before. If he didn't know better, he'd swear she was magic. If this was the curse, he'd take it.

Her hand ventured lower, lightly caressing his flat stomach and the indentation of his navel. Fingers itching, he reached for her, tracing his way along her slip, finding the hem, skirting under the lace to revel in the heat of her thighs.

As her explorations became bolder, he wrapped his hand around the fabric, drawing it slowly up, over her hips, along her stomach, peaking at her breasts.

She obediently raised her arms, and he drew the slip over her head, revealing the glow of her naked body, the pale, tender skin, impossibly pink nipples, her navel and the dusky whisper between her legs.

"Gorgeous," he managed, reaching to touch her. He could have stared at her beauty forever.

But her hands settled on his chest. She stepped in, and his view was lost. But one amazing sense was replaced with another as she kissed him. Her mouth was wide-open, welcoming him inside. His arms slipped back around her, palms dragging along her spine, to her bottom, where he gave in to need and passion, and scooped her up, spreading her thighs, pressing her intimately to him as their kiss moved to a whole new level.

When he finally found it in him to pull back, she gasped for air.

He braced her with his forearm, moving his free hand up her side, cupping it around her breast, feeling the beaded nipple all but scorch his palm. He caressed it with his thumb, and she moaned.

Feeling an immense sense of satisfaction soar through his body, he tried it again. She arched against him, choking out his name.

"Good?" he asked.

In answer, her thighs tightened around him, and she kissed him deeply. Passion pulsed through his body. He knew that if he hugged her tighter, just a little tighter, they could fuse into one.

Instead, he turned, easing down on the bed, Ann in his lap, facing him. His taut thighs took her weight, giving his hands full rein to explore her body.

She did the same, and soon he was naked, too, lying on the bed beside her. He kissed her neck, the tip of her shoulder, her breasts and belly, working his way down her body, tasting every inch, drinking in her essence, memorizing every spot that made her twitch, every caress that made her gasp.

Her hands and lips began a more thorough exploration of their own, until a roar started in his ears, and he swiftly flipped her onto her back. He kissed her swollen lips, and had a condom on in seconds.

"Okay?" he asked her.

Eyes glazed, she nodded.

Bracing on his elbows, he eased slowly inside her. He locked his gaze with hers, feeling her hot, tight body close around him. He gritted his teeth against the wash of sensation. He buried his face in the crook of her neck, inhaling the scent of her hair. Her long legs wrapped around his waist, changing the angle between them.

His pace quickened, and he sought her mouth, tasting deep, one hand moving to her breast, wanting to drink in every possible sensation. Her own hands grasped his shoulders, fingertips bearing down, small nails biting into his skin.

There was no Rayas or America, no statue, no crime, nothing but Ann, under him and around him, her taste, her scent, her small voice groaning a higher and higher pitch.

Though paradise beckoned, he held it back, his strokes measured until she cried out his name, and her body convulsed around him. He let go, a jet engine roaring through his brain, rocketing him to ecstasy as his body convulsed and he groaned her name over and over again.

The feeling subsided slowly, his iron-hard muscles releasing their tension, his lungs working overtime to replace the oxygen in his body.

Ann's eyes were closed, her body limp as she dragged in her own deep breaths. He stayed braced above her, smoothing the wisps of blond hair from her face.

Her eyes finally opened, meeting his in what looked like a daze. Then she smiled, and those blue eyes sparkled, and the most beautiful sense of peace came over him.

He kissed her lips, and she drew it out for a very long moment, until he pulled back.

"Do I get a gold star?" he joked.

She didn't miss a beat. "If I say no, will I go to the dungeon?"

He found himself sobering. "I'll never put you in a dungeon."

"That was a joke, Raif."

"I know."

They were both silent.

"You do get a gold star," she whispered.

He smiled again and gave her a quick kiss. "I knew I had it in me."

"Don't get all conceited again."

"Who, me?"

She smacked his shoulder, and he eased off to one side, moving an arm around her, cradling her against his body.

As they relaxed in each other's arms, he asked the question that had him curious. "Who was on the phone?"

Ann walked her fingers along his chest. "My friend Darby." She retraced the pattern back the other way. "It seems nobody noticed I was missing." She paused for a moment. "Wait. Maybe I shouldn't be telling you that."

"You're already free to go," he pointed out, smoothing back her hair as an excuse to touch her.

"Raif?" Her fingers twirled in a circle.

"Yes?" He splayed a hand over her flat stomach.

"What if it's not your statue?"

"It is my statue." Of that, he was certain.

She opened her mouth, but he silenced her by laying a finger across her lips. "Let's pick a topic where we don't have to fight."

She shut her mouth. Then she cocked her head to one side and narrowed her eyes, screwing up her face in concentration, as if she couldn't think of anything to say.

"Oh, give me a break." He nudged her with his knee.

"Darby and I are thinking of going to Vegas," she offered.

"Have you been there before?" He could easily picture Ann dressed up at a glittering, music-filled party.

"I have not," she said, and shook her head against the white pillowcase.

"There's a resort area on the Rayasian coast that has gambling," he found himself telling her.

"Seriously?"

"Absolutely."

"And drinking?" she asked.

"Of course. People don't gamble well while they're sober."

"I thought alcohol was illegal in Rayas."

"There's not a lot of alcohol consumption in Rayas, but it's not illegal. And the hotels that cater to Europeans have an international ambiance. You might like it better than Vegas." When he realized what he'd said, he shut his mouth. Was he suggesting she try the Copper Coast on her next vacation? Was he inviting her back to Rayas?

"You think?" she asked softly.

"It's a beautiful part of the world."

"Is that where you vacation?"

He settled more comfortably on the bed, pulling a quilt up over their naked bodies.

"Once or twice," he told her. "The family has a private island off the coast of Greece. We also like Monaco and Istanbul."

"Private islands there?" she asked.

"Just estates."

"Do you know how that sounds? 'Just estates.' Like an estate in Istanbul is nothing."

"You want me to apologize for having money?" Her attitude surprised him. She dealt with wealthy families every day in her professional life. Waverly's and every other high-end auction house would be out of business without them. Both the buyers and the sellers were the international elite.

"No."

"Then, why the snobbery?"

"You think I'm a snob, Your Royal Highness, Prince Raif and a-dozen-other-names with the palace, the private jet and the get-out-of-jail-free passport?"

"Yes, I think you're a snob for assuming wealthy people are different."

"I went to school with wealthy people. Trust me, they are different."

He was curious. "What school was that?"

"Hampton Heights private school in D.C. I was a day student. I only got in because my parents taught there. But my classmates had offshore trust funds and hyphenated names."

"And they didn't accept you," he guessed. From the tone of her voice, it didn't sound as though she'd had an easy time in school.

"They were mostly old money. I was no money. I had a free

pass to their world because of my parents. The first time I put on the uniform, I half expected to get arrested for impersonating a rich kid."

"I'm sorry." He genuinely was. Though he'd had the opposite problem, he understood what it was like to be ostracized. "I know what it's like to be different."

She turned her head, resting her chin against the tip of her shoulder. "Poor little rich boy?"

"I was teased and taunted and excluded."

"Because you were too good for them?"

"Because they assumed I was something that I wasn't."

She nodded to that, and he could see the empathy in her eyes.

"Did it get better?" he found himself asking.

"Eventually. It took a long time, but I made friends, and I did get a stellar education."

"One of the things I liked best about Britain," he told her, "is that they're obsessed with their own royal family. They didn't give one whit about the prince of what they consider to be some obscure country. It was nice to have anonymity for a change."

"I could sure use a little anonymity also, about now," Ann added.

He smoothed her hair, loving the feel of it against his hand. "So you know, I don't talk to reporters."

She brushed her lips against his shoulder as she spoke. "It doesn't matter. They make it up as they go along."

"Nobody knows you're with me."

"Unless staff at the Plaza talked."

"Jordan chose it because they're discreet."

"Most people can be bought."

He grinned. "We'll both deny everything."

"You mean, we'll lie."

"Sure, why not? You've done it before."

"Only to you."

"You're telling me I was your first?" he joked. "I'm honored."

Her tone went thoughtful, regretful. "I was hoping you'd be my last."

Her words tightened his chest. He couldn't help but think about the obvious double-entendre. Her last lover? Of course he wasn't going to be her last lover. That was ridiculous. But he couldn't stand the thought of any other man holding her like this. She was *his*. Though he knew it was impossible, he desperately wanted her to stay that way.

His arm clenched around her body. He kissed her temple, then her ear, then her neck, and then he was kissing her mouth all over again, feeling desire and possessiveness build up in his gut. He knew it was pointless, but he wanted to erase every man from her memory and keep her from ever wanting anyone else.

The next evening, at their meeting with Roark, Ann realized, no matter what the outcome, she was having her last moments with Raif.

They all met in the abandoned warehouse on schedule, and Roark now dialed the numbers on the combination locks that held a steel case shut. It was rectangular in shape, about two feet long and about a foot wide and deep. It was heavy, a struggle for Roark to move from his SUV to the table in the old warehouse.

But he'd managed, and the locks clicked open, and Roark folded back the lid.

Raif and Tariq both stilled, while Ann stared in awe at the statue nestled inside. It was laid out in a precisely cut bed of dense foam, where an exquisitely crafted marble woman gazed up at them.

Like the *Mona Lisa,* the woman's expression was enigmatic. At first, Ann would have called it serene. But the blink of an eye later, she would have called it satisfied, even pleased. It was the strangest sensation.

Roark covered his hands in a pair of cloth gloves. Supporting the pure gold base, he carefully cradled the statue and lifted it to set it on a black cloth he laid out on the table.

For a moment, everyone stood and stared.

She knew the statue wasn't glowing. It had to be an optical illusion, a trick of the light. But there was an ethereal quality to the beautiful woman that defied explanation. Maybe it was the mastery of the carver, or maybe it was the richness of the mauve and gold colors.

"Royal Han marble," said Raif, reverence clear in his tone. "Nobody knows how he did it, but the carver, Saleh walud Rahman walud Kunya Al-Fulan, is said to have made every pattern in the marble a near match across all three statues. I've seen two of them side by side."

"Imagine seeing all three," Roark put in.

"That must have been a sight," Raif agreed.

Ann moved to look from another angle, and the woman's expression seemed to change again. She looked disturbed, maybe confused. It was uncanny.

"How does she do that?" Ann asked.

All three men looked at her.

"Her expression," said Ann. "It changes."

Roark squinted down. "It looks pretty neutral to me."

Tariq joined in. "I've always thought she looked resigned."

"Patient," said Raif. "I think the word you're looking for is *patient*."

"Can you see it change?" Ann asked.

"It's a statue," said Raif.

"Like the *Mona Lisa*," said Ann. "Only more so."

"That was done with paint layering," said Raif.

"I can't believe you don't see it." It was blatantly obvious to Ann. She moved once more, brushing against Raif's arm, and the woman's expression went back to serene.

"I need to see the bottom of the base," said Raif.

Roark nodded, carefully bracing the statue to lay it on its back.

Raif crouched, pulling out a magnifying glass, putting it to his eye and examining the bottom of the statue's gold base. Ann exchanged a worried look with Roark. What was Raif up to?

"The provenance doesn't lie," Roark put in. "I've authenticated every piece of it."

Raif didn't respond. Instead, he stilled. Everyone seemed to hold their breath.

After a few moments, he came to his feet, brow furrowed. He said something to Tariq in Rayasian.

Tariq rocked back on his heels. "That's not possible."

"See for yourself." Raif held the magnifying glass out to Tariq.

Tariq stepped forward to take it.

"What?" Ann asked.

Raif glared at her.

What on earth could she have done? She was just standing here.

Tariq crouched down, repeating Raif's examination. "Son of a bitch," he spat. Then he straightened and handed the magnifier back to Raif.

Roark put the statue upright. "I take it there's something definitive down there?"

"Each statue has a unique mark," said Raif.

"Disappointed?" Roark dared to ask.

Ann took in the two men's expressions and body language. Raif had been wrong, and Roark had been right. There was no other explanation.

"Stunned," Raif replied to Roark. "Let me see that documentation again."

"No problem." Roark stripped off the gloves, moving to his SUV and retrieving the manila envelope.

Raif spread the documents out on the table. Each was protected by a plastic cover.

"Princess Salima really did use it as a bribe," he said to

Tariq. "They never took it on board the *Titanic*. The guard Zaruri became very rich."

"Salima must have loved Cosmo Salvatore," Tariq noted.

"Love," Raif spat, "does not come before duty. What was the matter with the woman? What is the matter with Kalila?" His voice rose. "Do these women have any idea how much trouble they cause?"

Six

The next day, Ann was welcomed back to the Waverly's office like a conquering hero. Nobody knew about the kidnapping, but everyone knew Roark and Ann had confirmed the authenticity of the *Gold Heart* statue to Raif Khouri's satisfaction. It was being reported by the online press that the statue was a huge coup for Waverly's. The story of the prison guard's bribe and the star-crossed lovers dying on the *Titanic* was going viral. And nobody was speculating anymore about her relationship with either Raif or Dalton. For the first time in months, she felt free.

At four o'clock that afternoon, she popped the corks on a few bottles of celebratory champagne. People had gathered in the common area outside her office. Edwina and a couple other board members had stopped by. Edwina, it turned out, had spent the past five days in Florida with some girlfriends from college, explaining why she hadn't missed Ann.

Even at seventy-two, the woman was lively and energetic. Her husband had died three years ago, but Ann wouldn't be at all surprised to see her embark on a new romance. According to Edwina, Florida was prime hunting ground for gray-haired men.

Ann poured glasses of champagne for Edwina and the board; her assistant, Kendra; Mimi and Zara from accounting; Nora from human resources; three of the men from sales and even Zachary from the mailroom.

Ann raised her own glass. "To the *Gold Heart*. And to Roark."

"And to you, Ann," called Edwina with a twinkle in her eyes. "You didn't let the bastards win."

"We had truth and justice on our side," Ann noted.

"Not that it always helps," Edwina added dryly.

Everyone laughed and drank their champagne.

Ann's phone rang from inside her office. Amongst the laughter and good-natured joking, she ducked away to answer it.

"Ann Richardson," she said as a greeting.

"Ms. Richardson?" The woman's voice on the other end was vaguely familiar.

"Yes?"

"This is Agent Heidi Shaw from Interpol's New York office."

Ann gulped, glancing at her champagne, wondering for a split second if she was breaking some kind of law. "Yes?" she said, not liking that Interpol was still flirting around her life.

"I spoke with Raif Khouri this morning."

The statement took Ann by surprise. "I see," she responded carefully.

"As you're now aware, it seems you were right about the statue."

Ann had known that all along. "Are you calling to apologize?"

"No. Well. Yes, sure, I can admit I was wrong. And I'm sorry I was wrong about you."

Ann set down her glass. The party was still going on outside, so she turned her back to dampen the noise. She was annoyed with Heidi Shaw, and she was tired of moderating her opinion. "Are you sorry because it messed with your career trajectory, or are you sorry that you inconvenienced an innocent woman?"

There was a small pause before Heidi spoke. "I inconvenience innocent people all the time. It's the nature of the job."

"You don't sound particularly apologetic."

Ann could almost hear Heidi shrug.

"I can't spend my entire life being sorry. You were a suspect. I asked you some questions."

"I think the word you're looking for is *interrogated.*"

"Maybe so."

"Why are you calling, Heidi?"

"Something you said during the…interrogation."

Ann sighed and drained her glass. "Did I incriminate myself? Are you going to arrest me again?"

"Not today." Heidi waited a moment. "That was a joke."

"You have a sense of humor?"

"Yes." Heidi's tone softened, making her sound much more human.

Ann was surprised. But she didn't suppose it mattered. "Okay. What did I say that interests you?"

"You said it wasn't you, and it wasn't Roark, and if I wanted to solve the big, international case, I should stop focusing on you two."

"And now you know I'm right."

"Even then, I definitely allowed for the possibility."

Ann was surprised to hear that, but it was good to know some law-enforcement officials had open minds.

"I've been sniffing around since our initial conversation," Heidi continued.

She had Ann's full attention. "Did you find something? Do you know who did it?"

Despite everything, Ann wanted Raif to get justice, to find his statue.

"I don't. Not yet. But there are far too many things in this mess that are coincidental. And they seem to revolve around you. You swore you never had an affair with Dalton Rothschild."

"That's because I didn't."

"If that's true—"

"*If* that's true?" Had Ann not established her credibility by now? "It's true all right."

Heidi was silent for a moment. "You're under no obligation to answer this, Ann."

"Why, thank you."

"Did you reject Dalton sexually?"

Ann's first reaction was that it was none of Agent Shaw's business who she did or did not reject sexually. But then she reminded herself that Heidi was only doing her job. She'd had no way of knowing back then that Ann was innocent. And she seemed like a fairly reasonable person now.

"I did," Ann admitted. "I thought we were friends, but he wanted to take it further. When I said no, it got ugly."

"Would you speculate as to why? I'm sorry, I don't know how to be delicate in this. Truth is, I'm not much good at delicate in any circumstance."

Ann couldn't help but smile at the woman's confession.

"Do you think he was seriously attracted to you, and your rejection upset him? Or do you think his ego couldn't take rejection from anyone? Or do you think the whole relationship between the two of you might have been a ruse, orchestrated by Dalton as part of a larger plot?"

Ann had to admire Heidi's cold, logical brain. "You mean he never liked me in the first place? He just strung me along?"

"Men fake romance all the time. Usually, it's to get a woman in bed. But it's a tried and true manipulative technique."

"I think he liked me," Ann answered honestly. "We have a lot in common with our jobs. We have similar likes and dislikes, and a shared sense of humor. It was when I wouldn't take it to the next level that things got ugly."

"Mmm-hmm," Heidi murmured. "Okay, one more tough question."

"Go ahead." Ann watched the staff trickle out of the office. A few of them gave her waves and smiles, and she waved back.

"How would you feel if you knew you'd been duped?"

A sick feeling congealed in the pit of Ann's stomach. "Are you saying I was duped?"

"I'm asking how that would make you feel."

"Stupid."

"Okay. Thanks, Ann."

"Wait a minute." Ann gripped the phone. "*Was* I duped?"

"I have no idea. I'm just trying to figure out if your subconscious would protect you from giving an answer that would shake your self-concept."

Ann hadn't completely followed that statement, but she thought she got the gist of it. "You mean I'm in denial, and Dalton was never really attracted to me in the first place?"

"It's possible."

"You're really not a fun conversationalist, Agent Shaw."

"So I've been told."

"What happens now?" Ann asked.

"As far as Interpol is concerned, the case is closed. The *Gold Heart* statue under contract for sale by Waverly's was never stolen from Raif Khouri. You, Roark and the company are all in the clear."

Ann's shoulders relaxed in relief. She gazed at her champagne glass, wishing there was some left in the bottom.

"But, if I was you," Heidi continued, "I'd be asking myself if your rejection of Dalton made him want to hurt Waverly's, or if you were part of a plan to hurt Waverly's all along."

Ann was glad she wasn't a criminal investigator. Thinking along those lines made her head hurt. Right now, she just wanted to celebrate. "In any event," she confirmed with Heidi, "it's over."

"Case closed," said Heidi.

"Well, then, thanks for the call."

"Thanks for the information."

"Happy to help," Ann put in automatically, though she wasn't particularly happy at all. Heidi had really put a damper on her day.

She signed off and headed back to the outer office. Everyone had left except for her assistant, Kendra, who was standing at the photocopier, back to Ann, pages chugging their way through.

"No champagne?" Ann asked.

Kendra swiped one hand across her face. "No," she answered simply, but her voice sounded off.

"Kendra?" Ann moved around to look at her face, immediately seeing her puffy red eyes and the streaks of tears that had marred her eye makeup.

Ann touched Kendra's arm. "What's wrong?"

Kendra shook her head.

"We're celebrating." For a moment, Ann wondered if they could possibly be tears of relief. After all, if Ann was fired, and certainly if Waverly's went under, Kendra would be out of a job.

Kendra drew a shaky breath.

Impulsively, Ann wrapped an arm around Kendra's shoulders. The two women weren't exactly friends, but they had known each other for several years.

"I'm fine," Kendra insisted, shrugging Ann off.

Ann took the hint and stepped half a pace back. "It's all over, Kendra. We're going to be fine now."

Kendra nodded, but there was no relief in her eyes.

"Is it something else?" Ann asked, reminding herself that people actually had lives apart from Waverly's. Ann's nonwork life was sadly lacking, but she realized she wasn't the norm.

Kendra's hesitation answered Ann's question. Something was obviously wrong in Kendra's personal life.

"You don't have to tell me, of course," said Ann. "But if there's any way I can help." She was thinking back now, asking herself if she'd been so hung up with her own problems that she'd failed to miss some sign from Kendra. The woman was normally an emotional rock. If something had her crying, it had to be serious.

"It's nothing," said Kendra, wiping away the last of her tears.

"It doesn't look like nothing," Ann responded.

Kendra drew a shuddering breath. Ann wanted to respect her employee's privacy. At the same time, she didn't want to walk away if Kendra was about to talk. She held her ground a moment longer.

"It's my sister," Kendra offered. "Roxanne."

Ann had never met Kendra's sister. In fact, she'd heard very little about her. She did know Roxanne lived upstate.

"Is she ill?"

Another hesitation, but then Kendra nodded.

"Oh, honey." Ann wrapped her arm around Kendra's shoulders and gave a squeeze. "Something serious? Does she need you? Do you need some time off work?"

"No!" Kendra's response was sharp and swift. "I mean, thank you. But no. She's getting better. She has, uh, friends with her. I've just been worried is all."

It occurred to Ann that the two sisters might have had a falling-out. Maybe Roxanne's illness was complicated by emotional issues between the two women. She decided it was better not to pry.

"If there's anything at all I can do," said Ann.

Kendra nodded, looking miserable. "I'm better with the distraction of work."

"Okay. That's fine. But keep me posted, okay?"

"I will," Kendra agreed.

"At least take the rest of the day off. Everyone else is cutting out early."

Kendra glanced worriedly around the outer office. "I don't know. There's so much—"

"Go," Ann insisted, giving Kendra a gentle shove. "I don't

want to see you back until tomorrow morning. And come in late. Sleep in for a while."

Kendra's glance darted to an open file cabinet. "I'll just close up—"

"I'll close up," said Ann. "We can make it a few hours without you."

Kendra was slow to respond. "Okay," she finally conceded. "I'll finish this up in the morning."

"Good," said Ann, watching while Kendra gathered her purse and shrugged into her winter coat.

Before leaving, Kendra closed and locked the file cabinet and secured the drawers on her desk. She gave a final glance around. "Okay then."

"Good night, Kendra."

Kendra paused by the door. "Good night, Ann. Thanks."

"I wish there was more I could do."

Kendra nodded in acknowledgement. For a moment, she looked like she might say more, but then she slipped outside into the office hallway.

The phone on Kendra's desk rang then went to voice mail.

There were a few clean glasses and half a bottle of champagne on Kendra's desk. Ann selected a glass and poured herself a generous measure of the sparkling liquid.

"Congratulations to me," she breathed, raising the glass.

"Hear, hear," came a male voice from behind her.

She turned to find Raif standing in the doorway.

"You definitely came out on top of this." He sauntered inside.

Ann didn't let his presence stop her from taking a swallow of the champagne. Then she lifted the bottle toward him in a silent question.

He nodded and moved toward her. "Not that I'm celebrating," he noted as she poured him a glass.

"You're not happy for me?" she teased, feeling strangely at ease around the man who'd once made her so nervous. She supposed it could be because she'd spent a night in his bed. Then again, that could have easily made things worse.

"I'm unhappy for me." He lifted the glass and took a drink. "You remember one of the first things you said to me?" he asked.

"Is this a quiz? And why aren't you halfway to Rayas by now? I'd have thought you'd have the Gulfstream in the air by lunchtime."

He ignored her questions. "When you came to Rayas last month, one of the first things you said to me was that somebody was harming both of us. You said that if we compared notes, we'd be able to help each other figure it out."

"I also said it was a one-time offer," Ann recalled.

"There's always room for renegotiation." He took another sip. "There was a time when I swore I'd never sleep with you."

"I don't remember that," she said, even as desire flared at the memory of their night together. She cooled it with another swallow of champagne.

"I swore it to myself."

"Clearly, you can't be trusted."

"Clearly." His gaze searched hers. "I'm here to renegotiate, Ann."

"You want to sleep with me again?"

She knew she should say no to that, but she wasn't exactly sure how she'd answer. Raif was a fantastic lover. She could easily imagine herself naked in his arms all over again. And, really, what would be the harm? He'd be off to Rayas soon enough, his mind occupied with princely matters, forgetting all about Ann Richardson of New York City.

Once his jet cleared U.S. airspace, it was unlikely he'd give her another thought. What did it matter if they made love three or four, or even five times? When it was over, she'd miss him, fantasize about him, get over him, and move on with her life.

"No." His answer startled her, and it must have shown on her face.

He quickly backtracked from the insulting answer, which

made it that much worse. "I mean yes. Of course I want to sleep with you again. But that's not why I'm here."

Ann focused on filling up her glass, telling her ego to deal with it. "My mistake."

Just because the sex had been fantastic for her, didn't mean it had been anything extraordinary for him. He probably slept with prettier, younger, more nimble and athletic women every day of the week. The past two nights, Ann had just happened to be the one in front of him.

Wow. That was humiliating. She slammed back a swallow of the champagne.

"It's been bothering me," Raif continued, perching on the edge of Kendra's desk. "All this time, all these months—in fact it's one of the major reasons I thought it had to be you."

His expression turned contemplative, his gaze going off into space. "Nobody's tried to sell the statue. Not a hint. Not a ripple. And Tariq is very good at sleuthing these things out. So, I have to ask myself, why the *Gold Heart?* There are many valuable items that would be easier to steal and to sell. And what's the point of stealing a valuable item if you're not going to sell it?"

Ann didn't have an answer for him. She didn't have the first clue about how a criminal mind worked. She did know a thing or two about the underground market in antiquities. It was thriving. And the bragging rights, never mind the monetary value of something like the *Gold Heart,* were immense. Raif was right. If a person knew who to talk to, complete silence was odd.

"If not for gain," Raif said. "That leaves harm."

"You think someone stole the statue to harm you?" Ann ran her mind through her knowledge of the *Gold Heart.* "The curse?" she found herself asking.

"There is no curse."

She knew full well he didn't believe it. But that didn't mean others were as skeptical. "If there was, how would it hurt you?"

"Ruin my love life, and that of my family, maybe keep us

from getting married, having heirs. Perhaps change the line of succession. But we need to be realistic. We can't waste any more time on dead ends."

"Unless the thief believed in the curse." Ann carried her thought through out loud, her brain engaging in the mystery. "Then stealing it to harm you would make perfect sense. Who would become king if you didn't have children?"

"My cousin Kalila would become queen. Her son then king."

"Maybe she—"

"No."

"You can't be certain," Ann argued.

"It would be easier to simply assassinate me."

Ann straightened in shock. "You think your cousin would kill you?"

"Of course not. Kalila had nothing to do with this. I'm saying, if the plan was to mess with the line of succession in Rayas, there are far more efficient ways to do it. If I'm the prime target—and that's a big if—the theft messes with my credibility. It undermines the confidence of my people."

He paused. "But don't forget the other side to this equation, Ann. You."

"Now, that's a convoluted plot." But it was more than a little unsettling that it had occurred to three different people.

"It could have gotten you fired," Raif noted.

Ann was forced to nod in agreement. Then she drained her champagne. "Like you said about yourself, there are far easier ways to do it."

He didn't answer, but his gaze told her she wasn't changing his mind.

She set down her glass. "You know, I normally lead a very calm, low-key life."

Raif chuckled, polishing off his own champagne. Then he checked the level of the bottle and filled both of their glasses. Ann wasn't inclined to protest.

"Seriously," she told him. "I don't know what goes on for the crown prince of Rayas, but my life is pretty ordinary."

He handed her her glass. "Don't be so smug. The one and only time I've been on the front page of an American tabloid was with you."

Ann waved dismissively. "That was an anomaly." At least, six months ago she would have called it an anomaly. Now, maybe not so much.

"Somebody's out to get you, Ann."

"That's a bit melodramatic."

"They broke into my palace, not an easy thing to do. They dragged your name through the mud, put your career and your company at risk. I don't know the book worth of Waverly's, nor the investment of individual shareholders, but it's got to be considerable. Who would hire you if you brought it down?"

Ann had to agree a hostile takeover of Waverly's had the potential to bring with it financial ruin for a number of people.

"Don't you want to know why?" Raif asked.

"Of course I want to know why," she found herself responding. She did. Who wouldn't?

He moved closer. "More importantly, don't you want to stop them from doing more damage?"

"But it's over."

Whoever it was had failed. The Waverly's *Gold Heart* was legitimized. Ann was in the clear.

Raif shook his head. "It's absolutely not over for me. I don't have my statue back. And there's the rather large matter of the revenge I'm going to exact. And, for you, if you're the target, they'll come at you some other way."

Ann's stomach went hollow, wondering if Raif knew something more than what he'd already shared.

"How?" she asked.

"That's the fun part. We have no idea. We don't know who they are. We don't know what they want. And we don't know what they'll do next."

Ann hated to believe him, but she was running out of reasonable explanations. Still, given all he'd put her through, she was under no illusion that she was his priority.

"You have no reason to care about me," she told him softly.

He straightened. "I care about Rayas. My priority is my country. And I strongly suspect they're still after you."

His words made perfect sense. She understood his reason for coming to her office, his reason for still being in the States.

"I'm the bait," she said flatly.

Raif's look was long and steady. "You're the bait."

Her laugh was a little high-pitched, and once again, she downed the glass of champagne. "You *want* them to come after me again."

He didn't deny it. "And when they do, I'll know who they are."

"Diabolical," she noted, thinking she wouldn't want to go up against Raif.

She'd been a bit of a fool to try it in the first place. The man was powerful, intelligent, cold-blooded and relentless. Then again, she supposed, with an entire country to worry about, he did have a lot at stake.

"Come to Rayas," he said softly.

She jerked her head up to stare at him.

He held her gaze with those dark, unfathomable eyes. "Come back to where it all started, and we'll follow it through."

"Why?" How could he expect her to do that?

"Because, when my problem is solved, so is yours."

"I didn't like Rayas," she told him. Not that she needed an excuse to say no. It was ridiculous for him to expect her to drop everything. And it was dangerous for her to trust him.

Had she known he was so all-powerful as crown prince in Rayas, she might never have gone to his country in the first place. He needed her now, but she didn't doubt for a second that he'd toss her in a dungeon, or worse, if she became an impediment to his objective.

"What's not to like?" he asked. "The weather is spectacular. The restaurants are good. You'd stay in Valhan Palace, be catered to morning and night."

"Until you decided to throw me in the nearest dungeon."

His expression faltered. "How can you even suggest that?"

"Because you threatened it on more than one occasion."

"When I thought you a thief."

"And if you think I'm a thief again?"

"I won't."

"You might."

"I won't, Ann." He set down his glass, removed hers from her fingers and took both of her hands in his. "Come to my country. I will protect you. I will treat you honorably. And if you feel a moment's discomfort or upset, I will immediately fly you home in my private jet. You have my royal word on that. My vow."

The warmth of his hands seeped into her skin. She felt weak, breathless and disoriented. She fought the sensations, knowing they were messing with her decision-making ability.

"Your royal word means a lot in Rayas?" she stalled.

"It means everything."

"I need to think about it."

"My jet is waiting."

"Now?"

"Yes."

"I'm not ready. I'm not packed." As she voiced the protest, she realized she was seriously considering his outlandish proposal.

Would going to Rayas flush out the thief? Were Raif and Heidi right? Was somebody still out to get Ann? Could Dalton possibly be mixed up in this? Or was this someone else altogether?

She realized she needed to know who had messed with her life. She was willing to go to some length to stop them.

"I'll catch up with you," she offered.

But Raif shook his head. "Whoever they are, I want them

to know we've joined forces. I want to make them nervous. If they're nervous, they'll make a mistake."

She withdrew her hands, struggling for some semblance of rational thought. "I can't just up and leave with you. I have a job, work to do, deadlines to meet."

Raif extracted his cell phone. "We can fix that. Who's your boss? What's his number?"

She didn't bother to mask her annoyance. "Is that how it's done in royal circles? Are you going to threaten my boss, too?"

Raif shot her a look of disdain. "What's his number?"

"I don't have a single boss. The board of directors as a whole are my boss."

"Who's in charge, Ann?"

She gave in. Part of her was curious to see how this would go. She braced her hands and hopped up onto the desktop, rattling off Vance Waverly's phone number.

Then she listened in astonishment as Raif made Vance an offer he couldn't refuse. If they'd let him take Ann to Rayas, he'd give Waverly's Cosmo's documents of incarceration into Traitor's Prison, signed by Princess Salima's father. As provenance went, it didn't get any better than that. The *Gold Heart's* value would go through the roof.

Done with the bargain, Raif put the phone back into his pocket.

"You are amazing," Ann told him, in genuine awe.

He shrugged. "I don't like wasting time."

"You knew he couldn't say no."

"That was the entire point. If you make someone a genuinely valuable offer, they don't say no, and everyone goes away happy. Come to Rayas, Ann. Let's put this mess behind us."

Ann wasn't sure she'd call herself happy, but she had run out of reasons to say no.

Seven

The air in Rayas was hot and humid, saturated with the scent of jasmine and a sticky salt-tang that blew in from the Mediterranean. Ann gazed over Raif's shoulder through the small doorway of the Gulfstream to the red carpet and the lineup of forty officials waiting to greet him.

"You have got to be joking," she muttered under her breath.

"He's been gone over a week," said Tariq from close beside her in the small airplane foyer.

"I could be gone for a year, and I'd be lucky to have Darby slow down for curbside pickup."

Raif chuckled in front of them. "Stop," he ordered.

"What?"

"Making me laugh. I'm supposed to look dignified right now."

She moved to pat his shoulder, but Tariq snagged her hand. "Not in public," he warned in an undertone.

"Seriously?" she couldn't help but ask.

"Seriously," he responded.

Raif started down the stairs, and a band immediately began playing.

"I'm assuming we won't have to pick up our luggage at baggage claim?" she muttered to Tariq.

"It will be brought to your room at Valhan Palace," he answered.

"I was making a joke."

"You're very amusing. Remember, five paces behind him through the receiving line."

"Wouldn't want to get thrown in the dungeon."

"Who told you we have a dungeon?"

"Raif."

Tariq grinned. "Then he's amusing, too."

"Are you saying Rayas doesn't have a dungeon?"

"In Traitor's Prison. But that's a historical tourist attraction."

"The rat."

"Who?"

"Raif. He lied to me."

"Probably don't want to call him that in public."

"Why not?" she scoffed. "Now that the dungeon's off the table, how much trouble could it possibly cause me?"

"It would be a serious breach of protocol. He'd have to kick you out of the palace. Probably there'd be pressure to kick you out of the country."

Glancing at Tariq's profile, Ann realized he was serious. He could go from joking to dead serious in the blink of an eye.

Raif reached the row of dignitaries, the first half dozen of them in military uniform. No women, she noted. As Tariq started down the short staircase, Ann tried to recall if she only had to stay five paces behind Raif, or if she was supposed to stay five paces behind Tariq, as well.

Taking a chance, she started down directly behind Tariq, not wanting to be left on her own to negotiate the lineup. Then she sobered as she watched Raif moving his way along the line. The military officers offered him snappy salutes, while other men, some in business suits and some in traditional robes, gave abbreviated bows, one or two of them exchanging a word with him. At the end of the line, two men took up positions on either side of Raif, speaking rapidly and flipping through papers as they walked toward a row of limos. The car at the front had twin flags and bright door seals.

She made to follow Raif, but a female military officer appeared from somewhere to walk beside her.

"This way, ma'am," said the woman, in accented English, gesturing to one of the other cars.

"I'm with Raif."

The woman frowned.

"I mean, His Royal Highness," Ann quickly amended.

"This way, please," the woman repeated.

"Can I at least ride with Tariq?" Ann wasn't thrilled about being abandoned this quickly in Rayas.

"The palace has arranged an escort."

Ann still hesitated. "What kind of an escort?"

The military woman glanced around, looking uncomfortable. "This way, please."

Ann felt compelled to give in. Raif was already in the decorated car, and Tariq was climbing into the one behind. It looked as if Ann could either travel in her own car or be left behind at the airport.

"Fine." She nodded to the woman, moving in the direction she'd indicated.

The chauffeur moved to the back door of a black SUV. Its windows were tinted, preventing her from seeing inside. The woman spoke to the man in rapid Rayasian. Ann could only cross her fingers that it was something good.

He opened the door for her. As she climbed into the seat, she realized she wasn't alone. She met the curious gaze of a young woman who looked to be in her early twenties. She was classically beautiful, with delicate features, subtle but artful makeup, a long ivory dress and a lovely gold, purple and white scarf partially covering her hair.

"Welcome to Rayas," the woman said in a lovely voice, with barely accented English.

"Hello," Ann responded, uncertain of what was expected, and starting to get a bit nervous about protocol.

"I am Princess Kalila Khouri."

"Raif's cousin?"

"Yes."

Ann was astonished. "They made you come to the airport to meet me?"

A slight smile crooked Kalila's lips. "I am here to meet His Royal Highness."

"Oh, right. Of course." Ann was growing even more confused. "But you weren't in the receiving line."

"Women do not greet."

"Right. Okay." Ann glanced down at her lap and swallowed. Maybe it would be better if she stopped talking for the duration of the trip.

"You may call me Kalila." Kalila's voice was melodic and regal, but also kind.

"Thank you. I'm Ann Richardson." Ann automatically offered her hand. But then she wondered if she was allowed to do that, so she pulled it back.

Unfortunately, Kalila produced hers at the same time, and Ann had to scramble to recover. It took a moment for them to sort it out.

"I'm not very good at this," Ann apologized as she briefly shook Kalila's delicate, royal hand.

To her surprise, Kalila laughed. "I don't expect I'd fare too well in Brooklyn either."

"You've been to Brooklyn?"

"No. Only as far as Istanbul." A wistful look came over Kalila's face. "But I hope to see America someday."

"Tariq seems to get there quite often," Ann responded. She realized women in Rayas didn't have the same freedoms as women in the West, but Tariq was a cousin—surely he could act as an escort for Kalila if she wanted to come to New York.

It wasn't as if the royal family had a shortage of transportation options.

"I doubt they'll be letting me leave the country for a while."

Ann gave a nod of understanding. "The British boyfriend?"

Kalila startled in surprise. "You know about Niles?"

Ann immediately regretted the admission. She hoped she hadn't gotten Raif in some kind of trouble. Then she wondered what exactly would get the crown prince into trouble. It seemed as though he was allowed to do pretty much anything he wanted, and the rest of the country had to suck it up.

"I'm sorry," she quickly put in. "While Raif, I mean, while His Royal Highness and I were trying to figure out who stole your statue, we had to share a lot of…" Embarrassingly, Ann found herself blushing. "A lot of information," she finished. "I'm sure he didn't mean to gossip about you, but, well, it was very confusing there for a while. He didn't trust me. I didn't trust him. And, then…"

Kalila blinked in obvious astonishment. "You don't have to explain anything to me. My cousin is free to say and do as he wishes."

"I didn't want you to think we were gossiping. He seems very concerned about you."

Kalila's shoulders squared slightly, and she folded her hands in her lap. "His concern is for Rayas."

"Well, yes," Ann agreed. "But he is going to be the king."

Kalila's lips pursed tight, her gaze stayed studiously forward. "I thought you might understand. I thought you would be progressive."

"I am progressive." Ann couldn't imagine anyone thinking anything else.

She found herself becoming defensive. "I hold down a tough job in a man's world. I live alone in Manhattan. I travel. I once slapped the face of the president of Elvio Corporation for, well, you can guess what for. And I sent the crown prince of Rayas on a wild goose chase to Santa Monica. Though," Ann found herself remembering, "I don't think Raif thought that was particularly progressive. Wait. I'm sorry. I meant His Royal Highness. Let's just say he was not amused."

Kalila giggled, covering the obvious slip with her hand. "I think I like you, Ann Richardson."

"Thanks. I mean, I think I like you, too." Ann found herself lowering her voice. "I have to admit, I like that you've taken up with that British guy and thumbed your nose at your family. From what I've seen, that took guts."

Kalila's smile faded. "The royal family will never allow us to be together." She looked incredibly sad. "In some ways, I wish the king had never let me go to Istanbul. It was easier before I knew what I was missing."

Ann's heart went out to Kalila. "Will things change after…?" She struggled to sort the words out in her head in a way that didn't give offense. "I know the king is quite ill."

"You mean, when Raif becomes king, will he accept Niles?"

"He might." When Raif let his guard down, he seemed almost normal. He certainly understood the world beyond Rayas. And he hadn't seemed to hold Ann's gender against her. She was pretty certain he'd treated her just as poorly as he would have treated a man he'd suspected of stealing from him.

Well, except for the sex part. But she'd assumed the sex was completely unrelated to the *Gold Heart,* and something Raif likely already regretted. At least, it seemed as if he already regretted it. He certainly hadn't even hinted they do it again.

"Raif will never accept Niles," said Kalila with absolute conviction. "I am to marry Ari Alber. He's the forty-year-old son and heir of an important sheik. Rayas must solidify our economic relationship with Brazil, India and Algeria. I can pout and posture, even rant until I'm blue in the face but, in the end, I will be forced to do my duty."

"You don't like him?" Ann asked.

"To be fair, I don't know him well. But he's stern and opinionated. He likes the old ways, and his mother—" Kalila abruptly stopped speaking.

Ann was curious, but she didn't want to pry. She guessed

insulting the future royal in-laws in front of a stranger could get dicey.

Kalila's future sounded terrible, and Ann couldn't begin to imagine the weight resting on the woman's slim shoulders.

They rode in silence for a while, and the beaches, shops and hotels turned to industrial buildings and the cranes and storage yards of a container port. The highway rose along a hillside, and they could look down on the semi-trailer trucks, heavy equipment and the rough-looking men operating them.

Eventually Ann's curiosity won out. "How will they force you to marry him?"

"I need the king's permission to marry, and he will not say yes for any other man."

"Because you're young?"

"All members of the royal family need the king's permission to marry."

"Does Raif?"

Ann didn't like to wonder about the woman Raif might one day marry. But at times she couldn't help herself. It would obviously have to be someone young, virginal, dark-eyed, blue-blooded and Rayasian. She wondered if Raif would hold out for someone he liked, or simply take the most advantageous offer. He certainly didn't seem to care much about emotions.

She reminded herself she should be grateful to know going in exactly how her affair would end. There was certainly nothing about plain old Ann Richardson that would benefit the crown prince of Rayas. Even if he had been interested in sleeping with her again, there was absolutely no future for them.

"For now, yes," Kalila answered Ann's question. "Well, he always will need permission. But when he is king, he would be asking himself."

Kalila's joke lightened the mood.

"I wish there was something I could do to help you," Ann found herself saying.

"No one can help me."

"Have you thought about leaving Rayas? If you're serious about this Niles guy, perhaps you could emigrate to Britain."

Kalila's smile was sad. "It is very complicated. And far too many lives would be ruined by my actions."

"But they can ruin yours? Do I have to explain how that's not fair?"

In this day and age, there was no reason for a woman to sacrifice her life for the good of other people.

"Is it fair that I'm a princess?" Kalila asked.

Ann didn't have a ready answer for that.

"The good goes with the bad," said Kalila. "But that doesn't mean I won't complain. I'm not going to make it easy for them."

"Good for you," said Ann.

Then Kalila pointed out the window. "Those are the palace gates."

Ann turned to see an expanse of polished white stone wall and an imposing set of wrought-iron gates. She sensed Kalila had said all she was going to about her future. And she found her stomach tightening in anticipation of seeing Raif.

There were days when Raif was weary of being crown prince. And this was one of them.

"Weeks," his father's doctor was saying, expression grave. "Perhaps months."

His worst fears confirmed, Raif wanted to forget about the constant parade of royal duties and spend this precious time with his father.

Able to hear the entire conversation, Tariq was standing near the door of the meeting room where Raif and the doctor sat at an oval mahogany table. Tariq wouldn't rush them, but Raif could sense his impatience. There were a couple of dozen people outside the closed doors in the antechamber, waiting for an audience with the crown prince.

"Is he in pain?" Raif asked.

After so many bouts of partang fever, it was difficult to believe his father would not get well this time.

"He rarely regains consciousness. And when he does, the nurse makes sure the morphine drip is at maximum. We are doing all we can to make him comfortable. But he is in no condition to run the country."

Raif nodded, the lump in his throat preventing speech.

"I suggest you speak to the chancellor today, about an interim—"

"No." Raif's answer was short.

"There are matters that need—"

"No," Raif repeated with conviction. "He is king. Until the day he dies, he is king."

As Tariq moved closer to the conversation, his tone was conciliatory, and Raif knew he was being handled. "We understand your loyalty, Your Royal Highness, and it is admirable. But there are matters that cannot wait."

"The king is dying," Raif answered coldly.

"Ari Alber's family is calling." Tariq stood his ground.

"I will speak to Kalila."

"And say what?" Tariq pressed.

"That she must do her duty."

"And, if she won't?"

"She will."

"You do love denial," Tariq muttered.

Glancing back and forth at the standoff between the two men, the doctor chose the moment for a strategic retreat. He stood from his chair and crossed swiftly to the door. There, he gave a small, quick bow before exiting, and the door swung closed behind him.

Raif knew he should rebuke Tariq for his insolence in front of the doctor, but he simply didn't have the energy.

"You need to warn them that she might refuse," said Tariq.

"And impact the trade deal?"

"It'll be worse if they're blindsided by it later."

Raif knew Tariq was right. He didn't voice agreement with

him, but he didn't argue any further either. He'd try reason-
ing with Kalila one more time before he contacted the Albers.

"What else?" he asked instead, referring to the crowd of
people outside the door. For the moment, he wanted to focus
on a problem he could solve.

Tariq appeared to understand. "The offshore boundary dis-
pute between Masuer and Geenan provinces."

"Tell them to share and play nice."

Tariq smiled. "Certainly. Of course. How could that possibly end badly?"

Raif brought his hands down on the carved, wooden arms
of his chair. "Concede to Masuer on the border, and then ap-
prove the money for the Geenan port expansion."

"Good decision," said Tariq.

"I'm so very pleased it meets with your approval."

"Don't kill the messenger," Tariq complained.

"We both know you can take it. What else?"

"Your uncle is shopping for support again."

"He's upset about losing his bride." Raif's uncle was a traditional man, and his pride had been seriously damaged in
the debacle.

"True," said Tariq. "But he's turned his focus on you."

Raif's uncle Prince Mallik had always coveted the throne
of Rayas. He'd once gone so far as to petition the chancellor to reenact a three-hundred-year-old law allowing a king's
younger brother to succeed if the king's eldest son was younger
than thirty. The chancellor had flatly refused, and Raif's birthday earlier this year had quashed even the faintest of Mallik's hopes.

"He's out of time," said Raif.

"He's spreading rumors that you're unfit."

"In what way?"

"That you're too Western. You've lost touch with your roots.
That Rayas needs a steady conservative hand at the helm."

"Are you worried?" asked Raif.

"I'm monitoring," Tariq replied. "Jordan has agreed to relocate to Rayas. He's proving very valuable."

"Do you want me to help worry?"

Tariq coughed out a laugh. "Not necessary."

"Good. What else?"

"The *HMS Safi* hit a reef off Australia."

That kept Raif's attention. "Is she still afloat?"

"Yes, but she's dead in the water. There's a possible fuel leak. Jacx is on his way to oversee a repair and tow it into port."

"The crew is safe?"

"Yes."

"You'll keep me posted?"

"Of course. So, Jacx is still a captain?"

Raif scowled. "You're starting to sound like the king."

"That's a bad thing?"

"I've tried to make Jacx an admiral more than once," Raif responded. "I can't force him to wear the stars."

"Technically, you can. But I don't suppose it would help anything. He is a good man."

"Yes, he's a good man," Raif agreed. "And we owe him."

Several months ago, Jacx had stepped in when Raif's distant cousin's groom, Daud, had abruptly announced a change of heart at the altar. What could have been an embarrassing incident for the royal family had turned into a celebration.

Personally, Raif had always admired Jacx a whole lot more than he'd admired the rather spoiled, shallow and weak Daud. And the moment Jacx stepped up at the wedding, Raif had realized he was the right man for Princess Salima. Daud was a fool.

"So long as you're trying," Tariq commented.

Raif didn't bother responding. "What else?" he asked Tariq.

"Five bank presidents are cooling their heels in the Seaboard Room," Tariq said, bringing Raif back to the present.

"Will the banking system fail if I cancel the meeting?" Pro-

tocol be damned. Raif was going to talk to Ann this morning.
Tariq and Kalila could chaperone.

"Yes," Tariq answered, his expression serious.

"Will it fail today?" Raif pressed.

"No, but there'll be a ripple effect on the markets. There
are already rumors about the king's health. Your attendance
at the meeting will provide reassurance. If you cancel, rumors will fly."

Raif stood from the meeting table, crossing to one of the
big windows overlooking the man-made lake on the palace
grounds. He let his gaze go soft on the colorful flowers, the
swans and the fruit trees.

With his father's health deteriorating, Raif realized it was
more important than ever that he focus on Rayas. But he
couldn't keep his mind from wandering to Ann. He'd seen
her briefly after they arrived last night. But they were surrounded by the usual palace crowd. Then Kalila had spirited
her off to a wing of the palace reserved for women.

Neither of the women had made an appearance at the formal breakfast this morning.

He'd never given much thought to his restrictive lifestyle
and how many people were constantly around him when he
was in Rayas. But now that he wanted to be alone with Ann,
he found it very inconvenient.

He could have called her cell phone, but didn't know what
he'd ask, to meet him somewhere, to sit down and chat with
him and twenty of his closest friends? And then what? They'd
have absolutely no privacy. Seeing her alone, in private, for
more than a moment or two, would break protocol and ruin
her reputation.

He should have appreciated it more when he had her to
himself in New York.

"I'm going to be doing a lot of that, aren't I?" he asked Tariq
unnecessarily. "Providing reassurance while people speculate
about the king."

"Yes," Tariq agreed.

Raif gripped the stone window ledge for a moment. He'd trained all his life for this, and now was the moment to step up. He couldn't let his infatuation with Ann or anything else interfere with his duty.

"Right," he told his cousin. "Let's go see the bankers."

Before they could move, the meeting room door flew open. Raif swung around, stunned by the unconscionable interruption, only to see six security guards barreling down on him.

"Captain?" Tariq roared.

"An alarm has been tripped in the south wing." Even as the officer in charge of the detail called out the explanation, two guards flanked Raif, grasping his upper arms, giving him no choice but to move with them toward the door.

"Ann," Raif called to Tariq. "Get Ann. She may be in danger."

Before Tariq could acknowledge the command, Raif was rushing down the hall with his detail, moving through his father's private office, through a concealed security door and into the narrow passage that led to a compact elevator.

Captain Ronshan and one other guard entered the elevators with Raif. The door immediately slid shut, and the motor whirred as the elevator headed down five floors toward a subbasement.

Raif gestured to the captain's radio. "I want palace guest Ann Richardson brought to the bunker." If this had anything to do with the *Gold Heart,* he needed to have her safe.

"Tariq will bring her," said Captain Ronshan.

"Confirm it," Raif ordered.

The man spoke into the radio.

Raif heard the affirmative answer crackle back. He gave Captain Ronshan a nod. "Tell me what happened."

"It was a third-tier alarm," Captain Ronshan told him, barking a terse order into the radio for the security staff to seal the palace. "The perimeter alarm did not go off, neither did stage one or stage two."

"How is that possible?" Raif was far from being an expert

on the technicalities of the palace alarm system, but he did understand that it functioned in stages. He'd been told it was virtually impossible for an intruder to get past the exterior system, never mind make it through two additional systems without detection.

"We're looking into it," the captain responded grimly, as the elevator doors slid open.

"The king is on his way?" Raif asked, pacing through the outer chamber of the bunker.

"His Majesty is under armed guard. We did not dare move him."

"And, if it's a bomb?" Raif demanded, completely unsatisfied with Captain Ronshan's answer.

The captain's jaw set grimly. "It's the doctor's call."

"Get Dr. Plare on the radio," Raif ordered. He wanted his father down in the bunker.

There was an uncomfortable silence while the captain exchanged a look with the guard.

"What?" Raif demanded, glancing from one man to the other. It was unacceptable for them to keep something from him.

Captain Ronshan flinched. "The stretcher will not fit in the elevator. It would be excruciatingly painful for the king."

Raif stopped dead at the entrance to the main room of the bunker. He turned around. "I am going back up."

"We cannot allow that."

"It is an order."

Captain Ronshan shook his head. "I have a standing order from the king that supersedes anything you say."

"You cannot stop me."

Captain Ronshan and the guard each grasped one of Raif's arms.

He gaped at them. "You would fight me?"

"We cannot put you in danger."

"The king is in danger." Raif couldn't let his father sit upstairs alone facing a possible attack.

Captain Ronshan stared unblinking at Raif.

The elevator door slid open.

With a burst of adrenaline, Raif shook free, only to stop when Tariq, Kalila and Ann appeared. Relief rushed through him all over again at the sight of Ann. He had to fight himself to keep from going to her and pulling her into his arms.

"What's going on?" she asked him, looking completely confused.

"It's nothing," he quickly assured her. "Just a precaution. Probably a fault with the alarm system."

There was a very real chance that this had something to do with Ann and the *Gold Heart* statue. But he saw no reason to upset her.

He looked to Tariq. "The king?"

"I ordered the doctor to put him in a helicopter. They're flying him to the royal suite at Fahead Hospital."

Raif nodded his appreciation to Tariq. That had been a wise move. If it was an assassin moving against the royal family, he would not find the king in his suite. If it was a bomb, the king would be out of the range of the explosion.

"I want to know the minute he's in the air," Raif said to the captain.

Captain Ronshan listened to his radio, asked for confirmation and then nodded to Raif. "They are airborne."

"Raif?" came Ann's shaky voice.

"Nothing to worry about," he told her again.

"This has happened before," Kalila told Ann, even as Kalila's gaze met Raif's. She knew as well as he did that the previous times had been drills or national and international incidents, like protests or riots that were far away from the palace. Rarely had something directly threatened Valhan Palace, and certainly not the inner perimeter.

Raif motioned for the women to accompany them into the bunker. It was three floors below the palace, surrounded by reinforced concrete, with dedicated power generation and communications systems, and an independent air filtration system. The structure was strong enough to withstand a missile strike, and storage areas beside the big kitchen held enough food and water for fifty people to last six months.

Ann gazed around the large open area that housed comfortable furniture, dining areas and office desks and computer terminals. The only rooms that were separate were the bedrooms, the baths and the king's private office.

"Are you survivalists?" she asked him.

"Only if absolutely necessary," Raif told her, motioning for the women to sit down on one of the sofas.

Ann sat, and Kalila took the place beside her. Raif chose an armchair at right angles to Ann, while Tariq conferred with Captain Ronshan.

"How long do we have to stay here?" Ann asked.

"Not long," Kalila answered brightly. "Last time it was a couple of hours, right, Raif?"

"Yes," Raif agreed, grateful that Kalila was so composed. He took a long look at his cousin, realizing for the first time she'd grown up while she'd been away in Istanbul.

Ann leaned in toward Raif, and he met her halfway.

"So, while we're here," she said in a low tone, "tell me what happens next."

"Next, they confirm how the alarm got tripped."

"I meant next on the *Gold Heart* theft. We need to come up with a strategy. I haven't had a chance to talk to you since we arrived."

Raif was just as glad to realize she wasn't worrying about the alarm. "Tariq has been asking around. He's looking for new contacts down at the docks."

"What should *I* be doing?" she elaborated further. "I'm really not sure why I'm here."

"I'm sorry about that. There were a few things that needed my attention. With my father feeling ill, responsibilities fall to me."

"That doesn't mean I can't help. Honestly, Raif, if I'm just going to hang around the palace trying on dresses, I might as well go home."

She had him confused.

"Trying on dresses?" His abrupt question drew the attention of the others in the room.

"Kalila insisted," Ann said defensively.

"She looks fabulous in silk," Kalila chimed in.

Raif could well believe that, but he struggled with himself not to picture it. He'd never felt an attraction nearly this strong to any woman, and it was throwing him for a loop. Ann dressed in the colorful, delicate, sensual silks of Rayas might well send him off the edge of sanity. He knew it wasn't possible for them to sleep together with so many servants moving around the castle at all hours, but he couldn't seem to stop himself from fantasizing about her.

"I sure couldn't wear them in New York," said Ann. "There, it's black on black, except for a few very formal ball gowns or at a costume party."

"We'll show you later," said Kalila.

"We need to focus on the *Gold Heart*," said Raif.

For a split second, he thought he saw a flash of hurt in Ann's eyes. But then she blinked.

"Just tell me what to do," she told him.

He spoke to Kalila. "Where can you take Ann to socialize tonight? I want word to get around that she's here, and that we have some solid leads on the statue's disappearance. I want to get the rumors flowing."

Eight

Ann felt beautiful in her Rayasian silk dress of sunshine-yellow, bright orange and deep red. But she couldn't help wishing Raif was there to see her. But, after the security team had given the all-clear, she and Kalila headed out alone in a black SUV with no one but security guards to keep them company. Raif had stayed behind with Tariq to hear details of the alarm investigation, and to do whatever other princely duties required his attention.

Kalila seemed quite friendly with the plainclothes guards. The men escorted them to the front door of a stone mansion across the street from a picturesque beach, seeing them safely inside a huge, octagonal, marble-arched foyer, where Kalila introduced Ann to an endless procession of people.

Kalila was clearly the belle of the ball, with people stopping them every few feet to gush over her as they made their way toward dining tables set up for two hundred on a massive terrace overlooking a vineyard. Dozens of local wines were featured at stations throughout a great room that served as a mingling area. They were delicious, and Ann began to sip her way through them while Kalila conversed in Rayasian. She stopped often to translate for Ann. Even so, it was almost impossible for Ann to keep up.

Then, during dinner, Kalila leaned in, lowered her voice and switched to English. She discreetly pointed out two men sitting a few tables over from the head table where she and Ann were seated on a raised dais with six other guests.

"Amar and Zeke," she whispered. "I've just been told that they bragged down at the docks that they knew who had stolen the statue. The story goes that one of the workers overheard them talking. The rumor made its way to Elena, the eleven-year-old daughter of a woman who works for Sheik Bajra." Kalila's lashes came down. "The woman on my right is, shall we say, *close* to Sheik Bajra."

Ann found herself glancing at the beautiful woman, and wondering about her romantic life. How did she pull off extra-curricular activities in a country as conservative as Rayas? Too bad now wasn't the time for Ann to satisfy her curiosity. "You think it was Amar and Zeke?" she asked instead.

"I think they know something that could help."

"We need to tell Raif."

"I agree," said Kalila. Then her expression brightened. "We can tell him now."

Following the direction of Kalila's gaze, Ann caught sight of Raif as he came onto the terrace. Those closest to him immediately jumped to their feet, standing at attention. Their action caused a buzz in the room, and soon everyone was standing, facing Raif, bowing as he passed by.

"I thought he wasn't coming," said Ann.

"Raif does what he wants," Kalila returned.

Ann craned her neck for a better look. Raif's gaze met hers, and her breath whooshed out.

He made a beeline for their table, the crowd parting in front of him. The second his destination became clear, five waiters appeared. Two guests, including Sheik Bajra's apparent mistress, were whisked from the table for eight, their dishes and settings instantly replaced.

Raif looked every inch the crown prince. He was handsome and very regal in a dark suit, a crisp white shirt, red tie and three heavy strands of gold braid running from an epaulet on his shoulder to the opposite hip. People greeted him along the way, and it took about five minutes for him to make his way to the empty chair next to Kalila. It was only then that Ann realized Tariq had accompanied him.

Raif sat down. The timbre of his voice was deep as he spoke. "Good evening, Kalila. Good evening, Ann."

She found herself inclining her head in a small bow. "Your Royal Highness."

When she raised her head, amusement sparkled in his dark eyes.

Well, what was she supposed to do? Everyone else had bowed and addressed him by his title. She didn't want to cause a scandal.

Thankfully, his attention was quickly pulled away. For the remainder of the dinner, the people at the table exchanged small talk. They listened to everything Raif said with rapt attention, no matter how inconsequential. The only person who challenged or teased him was Kalila. Everyone else was reverent and deferential.

After dinner and a few speeches, dancing began. Raif first danced with the hostess, while Ann found herself in Tariq's arms. But, very quickly, Raif was in front of her, holding out his hand, whirling her onto the polished wood floor.

The other couples gave them a respectful distance, so they were finally able to talk.

"You bowed to me," he teased, the thread of a chuckle running through his tone.

"I knew you weren't going to let that one go."

"Did it hurt?"

"It was a reflexive action. Everyone else was doing it. I guess I got swept up in the mass hysteria."

"Kalila was right," said Raif.

"About the dock workers?"

Raif and Kalila had spoken in Rayasian during dinner, and Ann had wondered what they'd said.

"What?" Raif asked. "No. About you in Rayasian silk. You are stunning, Ann."

She felt her chest tighten, and her tone turned husky. "You're not so bad yourself. You make a very handsome prince."

His arm tightened slightly across her lower back.

"I've missed you," he whispered in her ear.

"I'm staying in your palace." She couldn't help the edge to her voice. She was easily available if he cared to seek her out. "I'm sure you know your way around."

"It's not that simple."

"Yeah. I get it. It's a big palace, a lot of confusing doorways and switchbacks. And you probably haven't lived there very long."

"We can't be alone together, Ann."

That was patently ridiculous. "We were alone for days in New York City."

"Not in Rayas. We have to protect your reputation."

"From who? We're not in high school, Raif."

"The servants gossip."

"That means you can't talk to me?"

"If we were alone together, assumptions would be made."

"That we were having sex?"

It took him a second to answer. "Yes."

"Really? Nobody would be able to think of a single other reason we might spend time together?" She followed a few steps in their dance. "Nice country you're running here, Raif."

His tone went cold. "I'm not running it. My father is still king."

Guilt washed over Ann as she was reminded of the king's health problems. "I'm so sorry."

It took him a moment to answer. "Don't worry about it."

"I didn't mean to be insensitive."

"It's fine, Ann. I know you didn't mean it like that."

The song ended, and she expected him to step away. But he didn't. Instead, he led her into the next dance.

"Is this okay?" she found herself asking.

"What?"

"You and me, dancing a second dance. The gossip."

He seemed to have relaxed again. "I don't know why not. They can easily see we're not having sex."

"You've got me all jumpy about protocol," she complained, "and now you're teasing me?"

"I like teasing you."

"Yeah? Well, I'm not crazy about being your victim." Her heart and her mind were getting all muddled up when it came to Raif. She knew there could be nothing between them. But she missed him terribly when he wasn't around.

She needed to get away from him almost as much as she needed to stay with him, make love with him all over again. Forget her reputation. They could call her the whore of Rayas for all she cared. Nobody in New York City would give a damn about her sex life.

She wondered what he would do if she told him that. Then, she wondered for the hundredth time if he was even interested in making love again. He'd told her no in New York City. Before he'd backtracked anyway. And it didn't count if you backtracked to spare someone's feelings. But then sometimes she'd catch him looking at her, and she'd swear he was thinking the same thing she was—that she couldn't wait to be naked with him again.

But she was never quite sure. And now, as she glanced up into his implacable face, she was afraid to take the risk of asking.

"Did Kalila tell you about the dock workers?" she asked instead.

"She did not."

"It's a convoluted story, but two men named Amar and Zeke may know something about the *Gold Heart*."

"Is this the story involving the eleven-year-old girl Elena?"

"So you did talk to Kalila?"

"Not Kalila. Tariq already looked into it."

He'd known already? Ann was taken aback to realize he hadn't said anything to her. They were working together, and this was a significant piece of information.

"What did he find?" she asked, struggling to keep the annoyance from her tone.

"Nothing."

"How could he have found nothing?" It might not have been the breakthrough that solved the case, but it must have led somewhere.

"Elena is only eleven."

"So?" That didn't meant it was nothing.

"She wasn't credible," said Raif.

"Who talked to her?"

"What difference does that make?"

"No offense, Raif, but you and Tariq and, for that matter, most of the men I've met around here are intimidating. If you tried to ask—"

Raif frowned. "No men spoke to the girl."

"Who did?" Maybe she or Kalila could follow up.

"We spoke to her mother."

"Who spoke to Elena?"

"No one."

"No one?" What kind of an investigative technique was that?

"Is there something wrong with my English?"

"Why didn't someone talk to Elena directly?" It only made sense to Ann.

Raif stopped dancing, stood back and stared at her. "Because we didn't want to intimidate her. Have you been drinking?"

Ann raised her hand to thwack him in the shoulder, but then quickly thought better of it. She strongly suspected that kind of behavior would get her arrested. "One glass of wine.

The point I'm making, Your Royal Highness, is that if nobody talked to Elena, we don't know what she knows."

"She knows nothing."

"Because that's what her mother told you?"

Raif gave a sharp nod and drew Ann back into his arms, resuming the dance.

Ann was no expert on criminal investigations, and she understood that Rayasian customs and protocol were complicated, but she couldn't help but think it was a mistake to let this lead go.

"Do you mind if Kalila and I follow up with Elena?" she asked.

"For what purpose?"

"To see if there's anything the mother missed."

"That is not a good idea."

"Why not?"

"You Americans are the ones with the harassment laws."

"We're not going to harass her."

"No," Raif said firmly.

"But—"

"No," he repeated. "The last thing we need is you and Kalila meddling. Tariq has it under control."

"Meddling?" Ann demanded, jaw clenched in frustration.

"You don't know Rayas."

"Then why am I here?"

"To make the thieves nervous."

"So, I'm window dressing."

"Was our agreement unclear? You agreed to share your information and to help flush out the thieves."

"I thought I was here to help."

Raif scoffed out a laugh, as if that was the most preposterous suggestion in the world.

"Really?" she demanded, dropping her hands from him and stepping back.

"Ann."

"That's how little you think of me?"

"You can't walk away from me in the middle of a dance."

"Watch me," she responded, turning on her heel.

As she made her way from the dance floor, she caught Tariq and Kalila's twin expressions of horror. Maybe this wasn't the way things were done in Rayas, but it was certainly the way things were done in America. And what was Raif going to do, deport her? Okay by her. She'd even buy her own ticket home.

Before she reached the edge of the dance floor, Tariq laughingly twirled her into his arms. As she spun, she noticed Kalila smoothly move to Raif, repairing as much as possible the awkwardness of Ann's abrupt departure.

"Do you often save him from himself?" she asked Tariq.

"Daily," Tariq responded. "And, I must say, you make my job a lot more interesting."

"He was being a jerk," said Ann.

"He's the crown prince. That's his prerogative."

"It's annoying."

"Yes, well, do your best to cope."

"You're mocking me."

Tariq nodded. "I am, indeed."

"You don't even know what he did."

"Offended you in some way, I'm guessing."

"He won't let me help with the investigation."

"Really?" Tariq drawled. "His Royal Highness, with the entire Rayasian police force, intelligence service and military at his disposal won't take advice from a foreign auctioneer?"

"Rayas has an intelligence service?"

"Of course."

"And you can't find one little statue?"

The question seemed to trip Tariq up for a moment.

"We're working on it," he said defensively.

"I'd say you could use my help," said Ann as the song drew to a close. "And I'm not an auctioneer. I'm a chief executive officer of an international auction house."

The song ended, and Tariq drew back. "Thank you for the dance, Ms. Richardson."

"Thank you for the information," Ann responded sweetly. Her gaze was already seeking out Kalila. If Raif and Tariq were determined to stonewall her, perhaps Kalila would be willing to help.

Kalila had been willing to help, but it appeared Tariq was right. Elena had seemed confused and uncertain about details. The girl couldn't remember who had said what, couldn't confirm any names and wasn't even sure if the conversation she'd overheard had been about the *Gold Heart* or something else.

It was nearly eleven o'clock that night, and Ann's mind was clicking through the conversation, searching for tidbits she might have overlooked as she slipped into an emerald-green silk nightgown with a matching robe. The set had been a gift from Kalila, who'd informed Ann tartly that a Yankees T-shirt and a pair of plaid boxer shorts were completely unsuitable pajamas for a woman of any social stature whatsoever, and they certainly couldn't be tolerated at the palace. Ann had laughed at Kalila's outrage, but she had to admit, she liked the feel of the silk against her skin.

She rehashed Kalila's translation of Elena's words and the mother's interjections. Then Ann turned her mind to the expressions on their faces and their body language while they spoke. As she did, another memory surfaced.

There'd been a stern-looking man standing in the corner of the room during the entire conversation. Ann was growing used to the servants and security who moved unobtrusively through every room and corridor of the palace. But, as she thought back, she realized something had been out of place with him. He wasn't dressed as security, and he didn't have the demeanor of a servant.

There was a knock on Ann's bedroom door, interrupting her thoughts. She made her way through the opulent room, passing a huge four-poster bed, the door to a massive en suite, a burgundy, overstuffed furniture grouping that surrounded a low oak table, and the two marble pillars that delineated the entry area.

Swinging open one of the oversize double doors, she found Kalila standing in the wide hallway.

"Hello," Ann offered in surprise. She'd been expecting one of the household maids with tea or fruit. Rayasians seemed to have decided that hospitality meant a constant stream of food and beverages.

"Raif just called me," Kalila said, coming straight into the room. She was also dressed for bed, her lilac gown covered in the matching robe.

"Did they seem nervous to you?" Ann asked, her mind still grappling with Elena and her mother.

"Raif?" Kalila asked, stopping to turn around in the middle of the room.

"No, Elena and her mother. Did they seem nervous?"

"It was me," said Kalila. "My station generally makes people nervous."

"More than that," said Ann. "And that guy standing in the corner? What was up with him?"

"What guy?"

"The big, burly one. What was he doing there?"

Kalila shrugged and sat down, perching on the edge of the sofa. "I just spoke with Raif," she repeated.

"Oh," said Ann. "Sorry."

In Kalila's mind, obviously anything the crown prince had to say trumped all else.

"He wants to talk to you," said Kalila, something curious and secretive in her smile.

"About what?"

"He didn't say."

"I don't understand." Ann glanced at the grandfather clock in the corner of the room. "It's late."

"Yes, it is," said Kalila, expression open and obviously curious.

"I didn't think we were allowed to do that," said Ann, struggling to understand what was going on.

"Do what?" Kalila asked in mock innocence.

"Be alone together in the palace. Oh, wait. Are you coming, too?"

Kalila shook her head. "Only to show you the way. He asked me to bring you through the tunnels."

A shimmer of uncertainty flittered through Ann's stomach.

It was after eleven o'clock. Raif's request could only mean one thing. Ann wondered if she should comply or tell him to get stuffed.

After days of minimal communication and strict adherence to protocol to protect her reputation, he simply summoned her to his room through some tunnel?

"What about *servant gossip?*" she demanded of Kalila.

Kalila came to her feet and padded across the room in her thin slippers. "No one will know. These are *very* private tunnels. That he's asked me to show them to you… Well…"

"Means he suddenly wants company?" Ann didn't make any move to follow Kalila. If it was this easy, why hadn't she and Raif been spending time together all along? Why did they count on snippets of conversation on the dance floor, or in groups of people.

"Means he trusts you," said Kalila, obviously ready to staunchly defend her cousin.

Ann wondered if Kalila suspected Raif wanted sex. Then she found herself wondering if she was jumping to conclusions herself. Maybe he only wanted to talk to her in private. Maybe he'd learned something about the *Gold Heart.* Here she was, getting all snippy with him, and he might simply be sharing good news.

"Okay," she agreed. "Show me the tunnels."

Kalila nodded, then stretched up to reach for a decorative sword hanging on the wall. She twisted the sword's handle. There was a popping sound, and a small hidden compartment opened up in another wall.

Ann watched in amazement as Kalila moved to the compartment, set aside a jeweled box and pressed a button, and a person-size panel in the opposite wall slid sideways, revealing a dim stone passage.

Ann reached out to steady herself on a bedpost. "You have got to be kidding."

"We don't use them very often," said Kalila. "They're kind of musty and creepy. But our ancestors sometimes needed to escape from marauding hordes. You can get all the way outside the palace walls if you know what you're doing."

Ann wrinkled her nose. "Are there spiders in there?"

"Probably," said Kalila, producing a flashlight. "We'll walk fast."

Ann couldn't help but chuckle to herself. Somehow, she'd been expecting to be handed a torch.

"I was ten the first time my mother showed them to me," Kalila continued. "I was under strict orders to only use them in an emergency. But I sometimes hid on my nanny or spied on the adults."

"Did you ever get caught?" The more Ann learned about Kalila, the more she liked the woman. In other circumstances, she could see them becoming friends.

"I had a few close calls. I guess I'm still an unruly rebel." Kalila led the way inside.

"Only by Rayasian standards," Ann couldn't help noting. The passage was dark and narrow, with a low ceiling. The door slid shut behind them, but the flashlight cast enough light to see several yards in front. The air was musty and still. Ann stuck to the very center of the passage, keeping a sharp eye out for creepy-crawly things of any kind.

"By British standards, as well. Niles says our children must attend a proper British boarding school, so they don't turn out like me.

The words took Ann by surprise. "You're thinking about marrying Niles?" The admission flew in the face of everything Kalila had told her so far.

"He begged me," Kalila confessed. "I keep telling him I can't. But now he's…"

"He's what?" Ann couldn't help but ask.

"Nothing." Kalila swiftly shook her head. "It's impossible, and Niles has to accept that. Now, we mustn't keep the crown prince waiting. He can be a bear." She strode on ahead, and Ann quickly increased her pace to keep up.

Raif kept a nervous gaze on the panel that would slide open to access the tunnel from his bedroom suite. He was only half listening to what his executive assistant was saying, waiting for a place to end the conversation and get the man out of his suite.

He knew it was foolish to take the chance of bringing Ann to his room. But he had to see her alone. He couldn't face another night without at least talking to her, maybe holding her in his arms, at best making love to her.

He knew she might turn him down, might tell him to get lost, but he had to ask. If there was a chance she'd let him hold her one more time, it was worth it.

"A relatively minor member of the royal family," Saham was saying. "But the request for an introduction came directly from Buckingham Palace. And the Walden-Garv family does have considerable influence with Wimber International and Iris Industrial. I was thinking a private meeting, followed by a small reception, or perhaps a tea?"

"Sure," said Raif, more interested in getting rid of Saham before Kalila arrived with Ann than the details of any hospitality with British royalty.

That was assuming Ann had agreed to see him. He realized it could go either way.

"Which one?" asked Saham.

"Either. Check my schedule and decide." Raif moved toward the door, herding Saham in front of him.

"Very good, sir." Saham made a note on his PDA.

Raif opened the door to usher him out. "Who were we talking about again?"

Saham glanced at the PDA. "The Marquess of Vendich, heir to the dukedom."

"Fine." Raif ended the conversation, closing the suite door, just as someone tapped on the passage panel.

He quickly crossed the room. He maneuvered the secret levers, and the panel slid smoothly open.

Kalila gave him a quick hello and goodbye, disappearing back through the tunnels to her own room. While a bemused and very sexy-looking Ann stepped onto his carpet.

She wore a shimmering emerald silk robe. It gaped open at the neck, revealing a matching gown with a lace V-neck. Her face was free of makeup, shiny clear, pale as moonlight, her dark-fringed blue eyes set off against her blond hair.

His feet automatically took him to her as the panel slid shut behind her. He reached for her hand. It was cool, slim, delicate in his.

Neither of them spoke. She didn't smile, but she didn't frown either. His stomach tightened with anticipation. She'd once asked him if there was anything he couldn't have. It was definitely her. She was the one thing Raif couldn't have, and at this moment she was the only thing he wanted in the world.

"Do you know how foolish I am?" he found himself asking.

That brought a smile to her face. "I tried to tell you that that first time we ever met. What makes you admit it now?"

He reflexively smiled back. "I was just thinking, you are the worst woman in the world for me."

Her delicate brow went up. "Wow. Who doesn't like to hear smooth talk like that? What else have you got?"

He tried to organize his thoughts. "You're Western, you're blond-haired and blue-eyed, not a drop of royal blood, and you have no political value whatsoever. You're not even a virgin."

"I've always liked my blue eyes," she defended with mock insult.

"I *love* your blue eyes. I love your voice, your intelligence and especially your sense of humor. But I can't do that. I have my duty. A relationship with you, even rumors about you, would cause unimaginable chaos for my family. My father is dying, Ann."

"I know."

"I am going to be king."

"I know that, too."

"I must marry soon."

Ann sighed. "A young Rayasian virgin with a royal pedigree. I get it, Raif."

"I'm sorry."

She gave a short laugh. "Hey, you're the one agonizing about it. Don't be sorry for me. It's probably just the curse. Once the statue is back, you'll fall for a suitable young lady and live happily ever after."

Raif wished it was possible. If he knew these feelings for Ann would go away, he might be able to convince himself to tough it out and wait. But Raif lived his life firmly planted in the real world. The *Gold Heart* statues' luck was a myth, as was the curse.

His world lit up when Ann walked into the room. It dimmed when she left. He wanted to talk with her, laugh with her, even fight with her. He wanted to share his pain over his father and his worries for his country.

"On the bright side," she joked, interrupting his thoughts, "between now and when the curse wears off, we could indulge ourselves."

He struggled to understand what she was saying.

"It's not like I'm a virgin. So you can't exactly ruin me for my future husband."

Raif was stunned speechless.

Seeing the expression on Raif's face, Ann bit down on her lip. Obviously, her joke had fallen flat.

But then, he pulled her into his arms. His embrace was strong and secure, and she found herself molding against him. For a stolen moment, she blocked out the past, the future, any semblance of real life. For a stolen moment, she pretended it was safe to love him.

She tipped her chin, and he brought his lips to hers. His kiss was gentle at first, but then it grew deeper. Their passion grew, and he cradled her head, stroking his thumbs along her cheeks, her temples, into her hair.

"I can't get you out of my mind," he whispered. "I try. I fight it. I focus. But nothing works. I don't want to hurt you, Ann."

She pressed her palms against his chest, feeling his deep heartbeat through his fine cotton shirt. He wasn't hurting her now. Whatever was to come, he absolutely wasn't hurting her now.

"I miss you so much," she confessed.

He touched the bottom of her chin, tipping her head. "Will you stay? Sleep with me? Let me hold you tonight?"

She nodded. When the pain came, the pain came. She'd find a way to handle it. But for tonight, she was his, and she was going to love him with all her soul.

Raif lifted her into his arms. He carried her through the ornate archway that separated his living area from the sleeping area. His rooms were massive, even bigger than the ones she'd been assigned. The bed was a carved four-poster, with thick quilts and a dozen pillows.

Inside, he set her gently on her feet. Then, with more than a little impatience, he pushed off the multitude of pillows and threw back the covers, revealing crisp white sheets.

He straightened, facing her, moving in close, but he didn't kiss her again. Instead, he smoothed back her hair. Then his lips curved into a very satisfied smile as he flicked open the sash at her waist.

Ann's heart thudded hard. Her skin prickled with heat, and desire rushed to every corner of her body. Nothing in her life had ever felt so right. He slid the robe from her shoulders. The nightgown beneath had a low V-neck with intricate lace and spaghetti straps.

His dark eyes went black, and he eased forward, placing a gentle kiss on the tip of her bare shoulder. He nuzzled his way to the crook of her neck, using his hands to peel away his own clothes. There was something intensely erotic about being touched only by his lips.

When there was nothing between them but her nightie and his boxers, he urged her gently back on the bed. Then he came down beside her.

"My own personal fairy tale," she couldn't help but muse. The ceiling was domed, gilded with gold, covered in a mural. There were huge windows on three sides of the room, with views of the gardens and ocean beyond. The dressers, armoires and chairs were obviously prized antiques, polished within an inch of their lives.

Raif pulled her against him, spooning their bodies together, his big hand cradling her stomach, scorching hot through the thin silk. "I'm a man as much as I am a prince," he whispered against her hair.

"I wish you were only a man," she found herself responding.

He gathered her closer still. "Some things cannot change."

She nodded, drawing a deep breath, focusing on his hands, his lips, wondering where he would kiss her, where he would touch her. He was an amazing lover, and her skin tingled in anticipation.

She waited, waited a moment long, and a moment longer.

"Raif?"

"Hmm?"

"What are you doing?"

"I love the way you smell." He placed a light kiss on the back of her neck.

Okay. That was better. Here they'd go.

She waited. She wriggled a little. He sucked in a tight breath, he didn't make any other move.

"Uh, Raif?"

"Yes?"

"You're not kissing me."

"I know." There was a trace of exasperation in his voice, and she struggled to figure out what she'd done wrong.

The seconds ticked by, and her tension mounted until she couldn't take it anymore.

"Why not?" she dared.

"Why not what?"

"Why aren't you kissing me?"

His hand tightened on her stomach. "Because I'm not made of stone. You're asking too much, Ann."

Now she was thoroughly confused. "Do you want *me* to kiss *you?*" He'd always taken the first moves, but she was open to it if he wanted to switch things up. She tried to twist in his arms, but he held her fast.

"Raif, what's wrong?"

"What's wrong?" His voice was strained. "I'm holding on by a thread here."

"Why?" She stretched her neck to stare at him. "Not to criticize Your Royal Highness's gold-star technique, but we can get this show on the road anytime."

He stared blankly down at her. Then he blinked. "Correct me if I'm wrong. Oh, I so hope I'm not wrong. But, did you take me saying 'let me hold you tonight' to be a euphemism for making love?"

He had to be joking. She bopped him on the shoulder. "What else would it mean?"

A huge smile spread out on his face. "So, your yes meant… *yes.*"

"Of course I meant yes. What kind of a tease do you think I am?" Were they suddenly having a problem with the language barrier?

Without another word, he turned her in his arms, gathering her close and tight as he pinned her beneath him. His lips came down, kissing her deeply, while his hand found the hem of her nightgown, peeling it up, tracing the bare skin of her thigh, her hip, her stomach, his hand closing over her breast.

She gasped for air, her brain moving from confusion to arousal at warp speed.

"Too fast?" he asked, even as he stripped the satin gown over her head.

"Fast. Please. Fast right now. We can slow it down later." She'd been waiting far too long already.

Nine

At breakfast the next morning, Ann's skin still tingled, in some spots more than in others. But Raif had meetings and appointments all day long and into the evening, so she wouldn't get a chance to see him. She told herself to be patient. He hadn't said anything about her joining him in his bed again tonight. But he would. She hoped. She hoped very much that he would.

For now, she sipped her strong coffee, and she tried to focus her mind on something else—anything to prove to herself that she wasn't a lost cause.

One of the serving staff put an omelet in front of her, just as Kalila walked into the breakfast room. The room was open on one side, and the ocean breeze rustled her green print silk dress. Like all Rayasian women, Kalila wore a colorful scarf partially covering her hair. She'd tried to show Ann how they were put on, but Ann was a slow learner. She hoped she could learn how someday, because they were quite beautiful.

Kalila sat down at a chair next to Ann at the round table for six. There were four tables in the room that Kalila had said was mostly used by the women of the household. So far, Ann had only eaten here with Kalila.

A server quickly poured Kalila a cup of coffee, placed a white linen napkin in her lap and put a fresh tray of pastries within easy reach.

"Last night went well?" Kalila asked as the server withdrew.

Ann scanned Kalila's expression for salacious curiosity, wondering if she'd guessed that Ann had spent the night with Raif. But Kalila's features were carefully schooled.

"I'm not sure what you're asking," Ann said.

Kalila lowered her voice, leaning a little closer to Ann. "Last time I saw you, you were about to have a conversation with the crown prince."

Ann still couldn't tell if Kalila was trying to subtly ask about her and Raif spending the night together. She decided to play it straight. "He doesn't know anything more about the *Gold Heart.*"

Surprisingly, the answer seemed to satisfy Kalila. "I remember what you said last night. About the man in the room."

She had Ann's attention.

"Something was definitely up there," Kalila continued.

Ann cut into the spinach omelet with the side of her fork. "They were nervous," she put in. "I don't believe for a second they were giving us the straight story."

"Which means they were hiding something."

Ann agreed with a nod. "And bulldog-face in the corner was there to make sure they stuck to the script."

"It's a definite possibility," Kalila agreed.

Both women went silent while a fruit plate was placed in front of Kalila.

"We need to get to the source," Ann said decisively. She couldn't stand the thought of sitting here wasting another day waiting for something to happen on its own.

"What's the source?" Kalila used a small silver fork to transfer a strawberry from the bone-china plate to her mouth.

"I'm talking about Amar and Zeke. Or maybe their friends.

If we were in America, I'd ask around. They might have bragged to other people, or somebody might have seen something, or heard something."

Kalila shook her head. "That's not possible."

"That somebody might know something?" Ann didn't see why not.

"That you could talk to anyone who might know them."

"You already know where they work. Somebody needs to go there and ask some questions."

She found herself wishing Heidi Shaw was around to help them. Maybe she could call the woman's office and get some tips. This had to be investigating 101. "If Raif and Tariq won't do it, I will."

Kalila's dark eyes went round. "Amar and Zeke work at the docks, Ann."

"I know. Are there bars down there? Maybe diners or restaurants that the other workers frequent?"

"I have no idea. But that's not the problem."

"What's the problem?"

"Women don't go to the docks."

Well, sure. Ann realized wealthy Rayasian women didn't hang out at the docks. But with the right outfit, a head scarf and some makeup, surely Ann could blend. She'd seen plenty of women use their scarves as partial veils.

"I'd dress in plain clothing, something local. I'd blend."

"It won't work," Kalila insisted.

"We have to do something."

"No, we don't. You can't even speak Rayasian," said Kalila. "Many Rayasians speak English, but many at the docks do not."

"Send somebody with me, and I won't have to."

Again, Kalila shook her head. "There is no one to send. No one who wouldn't immediately tell Raif of your plans."

"Your personal maid?" Ann tried. Many of her wealthy friends growing up had garnered the aid of their personal staff members to sneak away overnight or for weekend parties. Their loyalty had been strong.

Kalila smiled sadly. "I would not put them at such risk. They would be immediately fired and banished from the palace."

"Of course," said Ann. She hadn't thought of that.

The women went silent, each taking a few more bites of their breakfast.

"Why do you care so much?" asked Kalila. "It's not your statue. It doesn't affect your life."

Ann dabbed her lips with her napkin. "Whoever stole the statue may be working with someone in New York to discredit me or even ruin my life. Raif says that if I don't find out who they are, they'll try something else. And he's right. I'm not interested in the statue. I'm interested in who stole it."

It was Kalila's turn to search Ann's expression. "You like my cousin."

Ann was through tiptoeing around Kalila. The woman had secretly dropped her off in Raif's suite in a negligee last night, for goodness' sake. She had to know what was going on.

She looked into Kalila's eyes. "I like him very much. Last night—"

"You do not need to tell me."

"But you already know."

Kalila hesitated. Then she nodded. "The crown prince may do as he likes."

"I don't have to remain a virgin," Ann found herself explaining.

Kalila's copper skin took on a light blush.

"It's different in America," Ann said.

"It's different in Rayas, too."

Ann's stomach clenched in concern for Kalila. "Niles?"

But Kalila shook her head. Still, the blush grew deeper. "He protected my virginity. He understood."

Ann put the pieces together. "But you made out."

"We made out." Kalila's eyes took on a telling shine, as she obviously fought a fond smile at the memories. "I guess that's a colloquialism in America, too."

"We make out in America," Ann agreed.

Kalila toyed with her fork on a blackberry for a moment. "There is one way," she offered, glancing surreptitiously around the dining room.

"One way to what?" Ann asked carefully, hoping against hope they weren't still talking about making out.

"I can come with you to the docks dressed like I belong," Kalila said softly. "I speak Rayasian."

"You *couldn't*," Ann responded in genuine shock, even while her mind whipped through the enormous possibilities that would come from Kalila's support. "Could you?"

Raif's day had been long, filled with interminable meetings and appointments. All of them were long-winded explanations of the pet projects of the petitioners. He had no idea why so many people insisted on laying things out as if he was in grade school. He was going to start giving people marks for brevity, or maybe he'd buy a stopwatch. He was giving serious thought to assigning an aide to do timekeeping.

All day long, he had battled the urge to search out Ann. Last night, he'd stopped himself from asking her to come back and sleep with him again. He hadn't wanted to make any assumptions or put any pressure on her. But now he realized his mistake. Instead of spending the day anticipating another glorious night with her, he'd spent it worrying that she'd turn him down.

She couldn't turn him down. He wouldn't let her turn him down. Then again, she wasn't one of his subjects, and she wouldn't jump to attention just because he asked. He'd learned that fact very quickly.

It was nearly six o'clock now, and he was hungry. He'd also kill for a martini or a shot of single malt. But that wasn't how he'd spend the next hour. Instead of eating and drinking, as he deserved after working so hard all day, he'd spend it with the marquess of Vendich. You'd think a crown prince could get a break in his own country.

The door to his boardroom opened once again.

A butler walked in as escort to the marquess, and Raif came to his feet to meet a tall, twentysomething, expensively dressed gentleman.

"Your Royal Highness," the butler began, while Raif half listened and wondered where Ann might be right now. "May I present Niles Hammond Walden-Garv, Marquess of Vendich."

Then the butler turned to the marquess. "His Royal Highness, Prince Raif Khouri, House of Bajal."

Raif met the marquess halfway to shake hands.

The man's shake was firm, almost challenging. And there was a dark determination in his eyes. Raif found himself cataloguing Rayas's recent interactions with Britain, wondering if something had come off the rails. The marquess seemed to have a purpose.

"May I speak with you alone?" the marquess asked without preamble.

Raif looked to the butler and nodded.

The man left the room, closing the double doors behind him. Raif gestured to two armchairs set at angles beneath a window, then wondered if he ought to put a table between them.

"I'd prefer to stand," said the marquess.

Raif widened his stance and set his jaw, mentally bracing himself. "All right."

"I believe I understand how you feel," said the marquess. "I know that promises were undertaken and plans were made. But I am here to speak with you man to man. And I'm hoping you'll keep an open mind about what I have to say."

"You have me at a disadvantage," said Raif, his annoyance at his private secretary and his aides percolating inside his head. If this was an adversarial meeting, someone ought to have briefed him in advance.

"In what way, sir?" asked the marquess.

"I don't know why you're here."

The man drew back, astonishment clear on his face. "How can that be?"

"Incompetent staff," Raif ventured, growing impatient with everyone involved in this little scenario. He had half a mind to call the meeting off and instead tear the palace apart in search of Ann and sustenance.

"I'm here about Lila," said the marquess.

The answer wasn't the least bit helpful. "What is Lila?" A British company was Raif's best guess.

The man's stance drooped ever so slightly. "Your cousin Lila."

"Kalila?" Raif asked, frowning his disapproval at the nickname. "Are you referring to Her Royal Highness Princess Kalila Khouri?"

"Of course. Who else?"

"Her name is not *Lila*." Now Raif wanted to throw the marquess out of the palace for insolence alone. But then it hit him. Niles Hammond Walden-Garv. "You are *Niles?*"

"I am."

"The *Niles*."

"I'm going to say yes to that and assume Lila told you at least part of the story. Though, judging by your expression, she told you enough."

"Do *not* call her that," Raif ground out.

The door burst open, and Tariq rushed in. "Raif!" He gasped.

Raif turned to confront his cousin, his tone cold. "Can I *help* you?" He was furious with the interruption.

"It's Ann and Kalila." Tariq glanced at Niles then began speaking to Raif in Rayasian. "They've been taken."

Raif gave his head a quick shake, trying to make sense of Tariq's words.

"At the docks," Tariq added.

Raif's stomach turned to ice. "How? Why? Where *are* they?"

"Jordan's men saw them, but only from a distance. They were disguised."

"It has to be a mistake."

"No mistake," said Tariq. "Jordan's men were watching Zeke's warehouse."

"Who in the hell would take the princess to the docks?" Raif roared. But he was already moving toward the door.

Whoever had aided them was about to be severely punished.

"It seems they did it alone," said Tariq, falling into step. "We think they left through the tunnels. Before Jordan's men could get to them, they were abducted."

"Where are they now?" Raif demanded, his anger turning to sickening fear.

"Jordan's man is following the car."

"I'm coming with you," Niles said in heavily accented Rayasian.

Tariq drew back in shock, while Raif glared at Niles.

"You will not," said Raif.

"He speaks Rayasian?" asked Tariq in obvious surprise.

"Li—Princess Kalila taught me." Niles ignored Raif's order and kept pace with them.

"This is *Niles*," Raif growled to Tariq.

Tariq gave Niles a once-over.

"He might prove useful," Tariq said to Raif. "They sure won't connect him to the palace."

"I'm not planning anything remotely covert," said Raif. "We're storming the place."

In the hallway, a security detail immediately fell in behind him.

"They're not going to let you put yourself in danger," said Tariq, glancing at the six men behind them.

"They're not stopping me." He turned to the men. "Support me in this, or be instantly fired." There was no force on earth that would keep Raif from getting to Ann.

Niles spoke to Raif in English, determination dripping from every syllable. "And you're not stopping me."

Raif didn't have time to worry about the Brit. Ann and Kalila were in peril. "Do whatever you want," he responded, continuing on his way.

When she regained consciousness, the first thing Ann realized was that she was cold. A second later, she realized her wrists and ankles were bound. She was also wet, lying on a wet, stone floor. Then her brain was filled with the knowledge that something had gone horribly wrong. She was immediately terrified for Kalila.

Voices around her were harsh and guttural, men speaking to each other in Rayasian. She forced her eyes open, blinking in the dim shaft of light that streamed down a worn stone staircase. She couldn't tell if it was night or day. The walls were gray stone, and she seemed to be in some kind of a basement.

She heard a woman whimper beside her and craned her neck to focus on the sound. She tried to speak Kalila's name, and it was then she realized her mouth was taped shut. It wasn't until that moment that sheer, stark panic overtook her.

She struggled to look around, desperate to know that Kalila was all right. Had the kidnappers recognized the princess? Was that a good thing or a bad thing? Would they let her go for fear of Raif? Or would they hold her for ransom, or harm her?

Ann focused on the woman who'd whimpered. She was up on a chair, though she was also bound, and her brown eyes were wide with fear. It wasn't Kalila. The woman's skin was white, her hair blond. But there was something oddly familiar about her.

Kendra? Was it Kendra? What on earth would her assistant be doing in Rayas?

Ann blinked at the fuzzy image, wondering if she could be hallucinating. She remembered a sting on her neck when the men had first grabbed her. That combined with the woolly taste in her mouth and the sluggishness of her brain convinced her she'd been drugged.

The voices suddenly rose to an excited pitch. Men shouted.

They jumped up and seemed to be running in all directions. A few of them grabbed guns and fired as bright flashlights bounced down the stone staircase.

Ann could only duck her head and squeeze her eyes shut as the shots and screams and shouts rang out. It was all happening in Rayasian, and she had no idea what was going on. She prayed it was the police come to rescue them.

Suddenly, strong arms grasped her, lifting her, carrying her. There was more shouting, but the shots had stopped.

"You're safe. You're safe," came Raif's gruff voice, as he held her fast against his chest.

Ann opened her eyes to make sure she wasn't hallucinating again. But it was definitely Raif who carried her up the stairs, out into the humid Rayas night. He took her across a darkened street to a waiting SUV. There, he carefully pulled the tape from her mouth.

"Kalila?" Ann managed to rasp.

"Tariq has her." Raif guided Ann gently into the backseat of the SUV. He shouted some instructions into the distance. She thought she heard Tariq answer, but she couldn't be sure.

Then Raif was sliding in beside her. The driver, separated from them by a glass partition, put the vehicle into gear, and they rolled away.

Relief and remorse combined with the terror that was only just barely ebbing away.

"You're safe, Ann," Raif told her again, pressing her to his chest to hold her with gentle care.

"I'm—" she managed, but the word sounded frighteningly like a sob.

"Shh," he told her, stroking her hair. "We're going back to the palace."

"I'm so sorry. Kalila—"

"Is fine. We've got her. She's not hurt." Raif worked on the ropes binding Ann's hands. When he freed them, the blood rushed back into her fingers, and she gasped from the sting.

"I..." Ann began again. "We..." She didn't know what else

to say. There was no way to apologize for having put Kalila in such danger.

Raif freed her feet. His voice went low. "We are going to have a very long talk about this later. But, for now, you're safe. Nothing else matters. Nothing."

He helped her into a sitting position and put his arms around her shoulders, kissing her temple.

He drew a shaky breath. "But if you ever, ever, *ever* try anything so colossally stupid again, I'll punish you myself. And I can do that," he finished gruffly. "I'm the crown prince."

"I'm so sorry," she managed to say again. "It was my fault. I talked Kalila into it."

"Kalila will have to answer for herself."

"Oh, please, Raif. No. We were trying— You and Tariq wouldn't listen. We didn't know what else—"

"Tariq's had Jordan keeping Amar and Zeke under surveillance for days."

Ann drew back, gaping at Raif's implacable face. "What?"

"Do you think we would ignore a lead?"

"You told me Elena wasn't credible."

"She wasn't," said Raif.

Ann's relief and remorse bubbled to anger. "You let me think you'd dropped the lead. Why would you do that?"

"The fewer people who knew the better."

"But this is me. *Me,* Raif. I'm your partner. Did you bring me all the way to Rayas just to lie to me?"

"I didn't lie."

"You let me think—" Ann swallowed. "You let me put Kalila in terrible danger. Those men, they—" She couldn't go on. Her hands started to shake, and her throat clogged up, and she couldn't breathe.

Raif folded her into his arms, holding her tight.

"They drugged us," Ann said.

"I know."

"They threw us in the trunk of a car."

"I know that, too."

"I thought we were going to die."

"Tariq's friend Jordan had men who saw it happen. They followed the car."

Ann couldn't stop shaking.

"We're almost back to the palace."

Tears leaked out of her eyes. "Thank you. For coming after us. For saving us." If he hadn't…

"Oh, Ann." He kissed her hair, his voice barely above a whisper. "What am I going to do with you?"

They went quiet as the vehicle hummed along the ocean highway. The dark water stretched away on one side, business fronts and streetlights rose on the other, creating a strobe through the interior of the SUV. Her clothes, damp from the wet floor, were seeping water into Raif's suit, but she couldn't bring herself to pull away. He was warmth and strength and security, and she needed them all right now.

He answered a couple of phone calls as they drove, speaking to people in Rayasian. They pulled through the palace gates, and her shaking finally subsided.

"Did they find it?" she managed to ask. "Was it there?"

"No. At least not yet. They're still looking, but I doubt the *Gold Heart* was hidden anywhere in that basement."

"Will the men you captured talk?" asked Ann.

"Unlikely. I'm guessing the ones who grabbed you were pretty low in the hierarchy. They'll be more frightened of Amar and Zeke than they are of me."

"You've been watching them."

"Yes," he sighed.

"Hoping they'd lead you to the statue."

"That's right."

"And I blew it."

"Kalila helped."

"It wasn't her fault. Seriously, Raif." Ann knew she could leave Rayas anytime she wanted, but Kalila had to stay here and face her cousin's wrath.

"You should probably worry about yourself," said Raif.

"You know, you have ridiculously underdeveloped preservation skills."

"I live in New York City," she said defensively.

"It must be an awfully friendly place, or you wouldn't have lasted this long."

The vehicle pulled into a big garage at the palace.

"Someone will bring you some dry clothes," said Raif.

The driver opened her door, and she straightened away from Raif's embrace.

"Don't move," Raif told her, exiting from his own side to round the vehicle and come to her aid.

The driver stepped back out of his way, and Raif gently helped her to her feet. A woman was there immediately, draping her in a robe. Ann was acutely aware of her disheveled hair and how her face must look, smeared with mascara and who knows what from the floor of the basement.

"Can we take the tunnels?" she asked Raif in an undertone.

"Sorry, sweetheart. But you're going to have to brave this one out."

As they started to move, Ann caught a glimpse of Kalila. She was surrounded by several maids who seemed to be doing their best to put her back together. Ann wished she could go to Kalila and apologize. But Raif was whisking her through the garage, down a hallway and up the stairs.

Raif had been assured that Ann and Kalila were bathed and comfortably sleeping. Although the search continued, there was no sign of the *Gold Heart* statue. And none of the men they'd arrested were talking.

Raif sat behind the desk of his private office, once again facing Niles Walden-Garv. The man had helped with the rescue, but had not been allowed to see Kalila.

Niles sat in a black leather chair while Tariq stood off to one side.

"I'm here to ask for her hand in marriage," said Niles.

Raif didn't hesitate. "No."

"I have my queen's permission."

"Kalila does not have her king's. She is promised to another."

Niles sat forward. "She told me they are not yet engaged."

Raif clamped his jaw.

"He disarmed three of the kidnappers," Tariq put in.

Raif glared at his cousin. "That is irrelevant."

"This man may have saved Her Royal Highness's life," said Tariq. "And I've been thinking this through."

Raif silently warned his cousin to shut up.

But Tariq wasn't finished. "He also has family ties to Wimber International and Iris Industrial." Both of the companies were massive financial conglomerates with huge influence over global trade.

"Whose side are you on?" Raif demanded.

"There are no sides," said Niles.

Raif turned his anger back to the marquess.

"We all want Kalila to be happy," Niles finished.

"Some of us want Kalila to do her duty," said Raif.

"What is her duty?" Niles asked reasonably.

"To put the family ahead of herself."

"As you will," said Niles.

"As I will," Raif agreed.

"With Ann Richardson?" Niles asked.

Raif swore he could feel his blood pressure rise. "Ann Richardson is *none* of your business."

"I've been watching you," said Niles. "Listening to you talk about her. Watched you ignore your own safety and the advice of your security force to save her. You're in love with the woman."

"Irrelevant," said Raif, even though his heart swelled painfully in his chest.

He knew Niles's words were true. There was no other explanation for how much he needed Ann, for how terrified he'd been when she was in peril. And how cripplingly relieved he'd felt once she was safe in his arms.

He'd fallen in love with her.

And he couldn't have her.

And he might as well be cursed for how badly it was going to ruin his life.

"You will be king," said Niles. "And that means you cannot marry an American commoner. I understand. But Kalila is unlikely to become queen. And I am not a commoner. Would you deny her happiness simply because you can't have it yourself?"

"Cease," Raif ordered.

"Wimber International and Iris Industrial," Tariq repeated, switching the focus of the debate. He obviously understood that an emotional argument was not going to sway Raif.

And it wouldn't have swayed Raif. At least not in the past. But then he'd met Ann. And now he knew. He knew exactly what torment he would visit on Kalila if he denied her permission to marry Niles.

"She loves me," said Niles. "And I love her. I have vast financial resources and considerable power at my disposal. Surely you realize how hard I will fight for her."

A polite knock sounded on the door. An aide cracked it open. The man hastily beckoned to Tariq.

Moving toward the door, Tariq glanced over his shoulder to Raif. There was a warning in his tone. "An Algerian alliance is all well and good. But this is Britain. Britain." He disappeared into the outer foyer.

Victory was evident in Niles's eyes as he followed up on Tariq's point. "*I* am Britain," he reiterated.

"She needs the king's permission," Raif warned.

The door opened again, but this time, both double doors were pulled wide by two military guards. Tariq appeared, his expression grave. He stood at attention for a moment, then bowed deeply.

When he rose, his voice was thick with emotion as he addressed Raif. "Your Majesty."

Everything inside Raif froze to absolute stillness.

"The king has died."

Ten

Ann awoke to the sound of horns over the city. Dawn was only just streaking the sky to pale pink, and cool air still wafted its way through her open windows. Since arriving in Rayas, she'd become used to hearing the horns at sundown. But this was the first time she'd heard them in the morning. And the song was different, somehow discordant.

She rose to a sitting position, raking her fingers through her messy hair that had still been damp when she'd fallen asleep. Her head felt clearer this morning. Whatever drug the kidnappers had used seemed to have worked its way out of her system. Her bath had been scented with vanilla last night, and the servants had disposed of her torn clothes, so all traces of the dank basement where she'd been held captive were now removed.

She shuddered at the memory. Then she remembered Raif's strength and bravery when he'd rescued her. Sadly, she also realized he wasn't through chastising her. She was willing to admit she deserved it. But that wasn't how she wanted to spend her limited and precious time with him.

She heard voices in the hallway outside her room. She moved back the covers, swinging her legs to the floor, expecting a knock with one of the maids offering tea and pastries. But the voices passed by.

Then she heard more people, footsteps moving fast past her door, louder voices that weren't in the usual morning calm of the women's wing of the palace. She shrugged into a robe and moved to her bedroom door, opening it to look outside.

The wide hallway was a hive of activity. People seemed to be rearranging the furniture that lined the walls. They were up on ladders, reaching to light fixtures, removing portraits from the walls, replacing decorative pottery with candlesticks.

Ann blinked, gazing one way and then the other. Did this have something to do with their abductions, or at least Kalila's abduction? Were new security measures going into place? There was chatter going on, but it was all in Rayasian. She didn't understand a word.

Puzzled, Ann withdrew to her bedroom, quickly washing up and dressing for the day. She chose a simple pink silk dress that Kalila had helped her buy. It was full-length, and the cut was loose, the fabric light, and it was very comfortable. She slipped into a pair of light cloth flats and padded out into the hallway, heading for the breakfast room to find Kalila.

The servants watched her intently as she passed, chattering to one another in hushed tones. All the activity had to be about the kidnapping. They obviously knew Ann had been involved. She wondered if the palace staff would ostracize her after this for having put Kalila in danger.

Down a few flights of stairs, she made her way to the breakfast room. When she arrived, Kalila was there. It was far busier than usual. Kalila was surrounded by three security guards, two of her personal maids and three other men who looked like the aides that helped Raif with palace business.

Everyone stared at her, looking shocked.

Ann came to a halt. Just how angry were they with her?

"Kalila?" she said.

One of the maids spoke in rapid Rayasian.

Kalila spoke back, and the maid cast her gaze to the floor. Then Kalila came to her feet, expression grave, moving to Ann.

She took Ann's hands in hers. "You must change your clothes," she instructed.

Ann glanced down at the pink gown, suddenly realizing everyone else was in black.

"It is King Safwah," Kalila said in a grave tone. "He has passed away."

"I'm so sorry," Ann blurted out, feeling like a fool.

She quickly stepped backward, out of the breakfast room, back up the stairs to rush down the hall, cognizant this time as to why everyone was staring and whispering. She'd disrespected their king.

No, not their king.

King Safwah was dead.

Raif was king.

Beyond her guilt, beyond her sorrow for Kalila and the Rayasian people, there was the one thought that echoed insistently through Ann's mind. Raif was king, and everything was about to change.

Back in the privacy of her room, she hunted for something black. The dresses she'd acquired since arriving in Rayas were all festive and brightly colored. Her best and only choice was the black slacks she'd worn on the plane from New York. She had also brought a dark gray tank top, and she covered it with a black cardigan.

She switched from the little cloth Rayasian shoes to a pair of black leather pumps. Only then did she dare venture out.

She realized now what they were doing to the hallway. Decorations were being replaced by the symbols of mourning. The horns were playing to inform the people of their loss.

She moved more slowly this time, back to the breakfast room, uncertain of what she should do.

It was even more crowded now. People were clustered in

conversations, maids were serving coffee and pastries, which nobody was eating. The chairs were all filled, so Ann stood close to a wall, feeling like an interloper.

Then, suddenly, Raif entered the room, followed closely by Tariq.

Everyone instantly jumped to their feet, bowing low.

They separated to clear a path between Raif and Kalila, who had remained seated. She rose, bowing to her cousin. "Your Majesty."

Ann expected her to rush into Raif's arms, for Raif to hold and comfort her, and for him to accept her comfort and condolences in return. But he merely nodded his acceptance of her greeting.

Then Tariq stepped forward and appeared to take control of the room. Ann couldn't tell, because he was speaking Rayasian.

Raif looked around the room, pausing for the briefest of moments when his gaze met Ann's. His features were cool, stern. There wasn't a flash of recognition nor a flare of desire.

He might as well have held up a sign telling her it was over. There was no place for her in his new world.

His gaze moved on, and Ann sidled her way to the exit. She rushed back down the hallways and staircases of the palace, telling herself to suck it up. She'd known all along it was going to end. And Raif had far more important matters to worry about than an American ex-lover.

Back in her room, she located her cell phone. She had a travel agent on speed dial, and quickly arranged a return flight to New York City. After the arrests of the kidnappers last night, they'd find or not find the *Gold Heart* based on a Rayasian police investigation. Ann couldn't help anymore. Not that she'd been any help so far. In fact, she may have blown their entire operation. The memory was sobering.

She pulled her small suitcase out of the closet and quickly packed her things. She didn't have a plan for a ride to the airport. But the few times she'd been out with Kalila, they'd simply walked through the front door and taken one of the waiting cars. Ann had no idea if it would work when she was on her own, but she was going to give it a try.

Case in hand, she found her way to the grand staircase. The hallway and the foyer were as busy as the rest of the palace, with people making changes to the decor. She moved unnoticed down the stairs, making it halfway through the foyer before Tariq's strong hand grasped her arm.

"Hey," she protested, trying to yank away.

"He wants to see you," said Tariq.

"He doesn't need to ask me personally. I'm already leaving."

Tariq nodded his acceptance of her decision, but began to propel her away from the front door.

"There's no need," she hissed. Raif should be with his family right now, his sister, the people he'd known all this life, the people who loved him and had loved his father. He had a responsibility to the Rayasian people, and Ann was an interloper.

She was a grown woman. She didn't need false, flowery words from Raif. In fact, she felt sick at the thought of a goodbye. What if she cried? What if she begged?

Tariq didn't bothering responding.

She renewed her struggled to get free. "Tell him you couldn't find me."

"Lie to my king?" Tariq scoffed.

"Lie to my lover," Ann retorted. "Ex-lover. Please, Tariq, this will only be embarrassing for both of us."

"He wants to see you," Tariq repeated.

"Doesn't he have more important things to do?"

"Many."

"Then let him do them. You're his friend, his advisor, Tariq."

Tariq nodded. But then he opened a door in front of them, propelling her inside the dim room, closing it behind her, while he stayed outside in the hall.

Ann blinked to adjust her eyes. As she did, Raif moved

toward her in the small parlor, skirting a pair of armchairs to meet her by the door.

Her throat went dry at the sight of him. "I'm so sorry, Raif" was all she could manage. "So sorry for your loss."

"You were going to leave? Without saying goodbye?"

She adjusted her grip on the suitcase. "You seemed busy."

He removed the suitcase from her hand, setting it down on the floor beside them. "That's no excuse."

"I don't want to get in the way, Raif."

"You were never in the way." He paused. "Okay, you were pretty much always in the way. But that doesn't mean you can leave without goodbye."

"So, you agree I have to leave?" The moment the words were out, she regretted them. She wasn't begging, but she was definitely hinting.

He took her hands, and the sensation of his touch rushed like wildfire through her body. She was forced to fight tears of regret. This was the last time he was ever going to touch her. Likely, it was the last time she would ever see him.

"The risk is too high," he whispered.

She nodded. Of course it was too high. The king of Rayas couldn't have an American lover.

"I have a funeral to plan," he said.

She nodded. She knew how much he'd loved the king. And she thought she understood at least part of the burden that had just come down on his shoulders.

"It is I who am sorry." He moved closer. "I would give anything right now to be just a man. If I could, I'd give it all up to spend my life with you."

Ann blinked rapidly, eyes burning, shaking her head. "You don't have to let me down easy."

He gave a cold chuckle. "I'm letting us both down hard. I love you, Ann."

She felt as if a dagger had just stabbed its way into her heart. "No."

"*Yes.* And I know you love me. You don't have to say it for it to be true."

She swallowed, and a tear dropped from her lash, dampening her cheek. "I do love you, Raif."

His arms circled her, pulling her tight against him. "I'll never forget you."

"Nor I you." She would love him forever. The pain from her broken heart would never go away.

He kissed her then, a long, soulful kiss, one that was painfully, clearly goodbye. It made her throat ache and her chest burn. Too soon, he broke it off.

"I'm sorry about last night," she whispered.

"We'll keep looking. I'll— Tariq will keep you posted. If we find them, you'll hear about it."

"I'd appreciate that." Resting her hands against his chest for a final moment, she forced herself to take a step back.

His expression was haunted as he dropped his arms to his side. "Ann."

"You have your duty," she managed to say. "Maybe if I wasn't so blue-eyed, promiscuous, old and American—"

"You're not old. And I love your blue eyes."

"But it can never be."

He stared at her in silence. "It can never be."

She leaned down and lifted her suitcase. "You are an amazing man, Raif Khouri. Rayas is lucky to have you as their king."

Before he could respond, she turned away, groping for the doorknob, opening the heavy door to find Tariq standing guard.

"Can you get me a car?" she asked in a choked voice, as she walked blindly passed.

"Of course." Tariq fell into step. "We will take you home safely, Ann."

In Raif's office in Valhan Palace, Kalila sat across the desk, her head bent, her eyes downcast, face mostly screened by the black lace headscarf draped over her dark hair. As angry as he had been with her last night, Raif hated to see her like this. She was an intelligent, vibrant and spirited woman. He hated that he'd been an instrument of her defeat.

"I am ready," she told him, raising her chin, expression calm, eyes fixed forward.

"To be first in line for the throne?" he asked.

She shook her head, then stopped herself. "Yes. I am ready for that. But I am also ready to do my duty." She took what appeared to be a bracing breath. "I will marry Ari."

"That's good news," said Raif. "For me. For Rayas."

"Yes," Kalila agreed.

"Not so good for you."

She didn't respond. Though her eyes took on a suspicious sheen.

"And not so good for the Marquess of Vendich," Raif finished.

Her jaw dropped open. "How did you…"

"He came to me."

Kalila's hands tightened together in her lap. "He promised he would not."

"I guess he lied. He came to me last night."

Her head jerked up. "What?"

"He helped us rescue you."

"He is here?"

"He is here," Raif confirmed.

Kalila glanced behind her, and for a second Raif expected her to bolt for the door in search of Niles.

"I am sorry," she said instead, turning back to Raif, her shoulders slumping. "He should not have done that."

"He asked for your hand in marriage. Or rather, he demanded your hand in marriage."

"He is determined," Kalila agreed.

"He said you loved him."

She met Raif's gaze head on. "I do love him."

"But you will marry Ari instead."

It took a split second for Kalila's nod to begin. "I know my duty."

"And I know mine." Raif rose, moving around the desk, sitting in the chair that was twin to Kalila's. "My duty, cousin, is to take care of you and all other Rayasians."

She nodded her agreement.

"How shall I take care of you?" he asked softly.

She seemed confused by the question.

"Shall I marry you off to a man twice your age? Make you miserable? Force you to sacrifice your life for the good of your country?"

Her brow furrowed.

"Or shall I care for you by ensuring your happiness?"

"Your Majesty?" Her voice was choked.

"You can marry the Marquess of Vendich, Kalila. I give you my permission as king."

It seemed to take a moment for his words to penetrate. But they did, and tears spilled from her eyes, and Raif felt his chest swell with joy.

"Thank you." She hesitated for a split second, but then she rushed to him, wrapping her arms around him in gratitude.

Raif hugged her back, her tears dampening his cheek.

"Don't be too grateful," he warned gruffly. "Vendich threatened to make my life miserable in order to get you. This is partly self-preservation. And an alliance with the British is even better for Rayas than an alliance with Algeria."

"It doesn't matter," she cried, pulling back. "Nothing matters. You are the most marvelous cousin, and the very best king."

"Tariq?" Raif called over his shoulder.

The office door opened, revealing Vendich.

Kalila squealed with joy, launching herself from Raif to dash across the room.

Niles wrapped her tightly in his arms. His gaze met Raif's in a moment of gratitude and shared understanding, but then his attention was all for Kalila.

As the two left the room, arm in arm, Tariq entered.

"A royal wedding," he observed. "It will be a boost to your subjects."

"It will," Raif agreed, though Kalila's happiness was more important to him.

"Takes the pressure off you for the moment," said Tariq.

Raif shot his cousin a questioning glance.

"Kalila has bought you some time. But your subjects will want a queen. And you will need heirs." As always, Tariq was blunt. "Shall I start a list?"

Raif had to stop himself from shouting *no*. He didn't want a queen. He wanted Ann. But he couldn't have Ann. And especially in the light of Kalila's offer to sacrifice herself, Raif refused to give in to self-pity.

"Start a list," he told Tariq.

"Your Majesty," called a female voice in the wide palace hall.

Tariq and Raif both turned in surprise at the breach of protocol.

"She is awake," called the bustling female servant.

"Who is awake?" asked Raif.

"The European woman from the docks. I believe she's speaking English."

Raif and Tariq glanced at each other. A non-Rayasian woman had been rescued two nights ago along with Ann and Kalila. She'd been hit on the head, and the doctor had been monitoring her in a guest chamber at the palace ever since.

"Take us to her," said Raif, and the two men followed the servant down one floor and through the garden.

The young blond woman was pale against the white sheets, her chest rising and falling as she breathed, eyes fearful.

"Do you speak English?" Raif asked. "Français? Español?"

"English," she choked out.

"Do you remember the rescue?" asked Tariq.

She nodded shakily.

"You're safe now," he told her. "You're in the palace."

"I want to go home." Her accent didn't sound British.

"What's your name?" asked Raif.

"Roxanne Darling. Please let me go home."

"Of course we'll get you home, Roxanne," said Raif. "Where is home?"

"New York City."

Raif felt a stirring of unease, as his instincts came on alert. "You're an American?"

"Yes."

"And were being held in Rayas?"

"Yes."

Could it possibly be a coincidence? Raif still didn't believe in them. "Do you happen to know Ann Richardson?"

"My sister Kendra works for her."

"And what were you doing in my country?" Raif's instincts went into full on warning mode.

Her face screwed up in obvious frustration. "I was *kidnapped*."

"I mean before you were kidnapped. Why did you come to Rayas?"

"I was brought to Rayas by my kidnappers."

Raif and Tariq were shocked to silence. Roxanne's kidnapping had to be connected to the *Gold Heart* theft.

Something creaked in the corner, and Raif glanced up. There was a small, subtle movement in the wall.

Tariq saw it, too, and moved like a flash. He flung open the secret door, snagging someone on the other side.

The scuffle was brief, and then he dragged a man into the room.

The woman in the bed cringed in fear, cowering as if she expected to be hit.

Raif gaped in astonishment at his uncle, Prince Mallik.

Mallik's gaze on Roxanne was pure poison.

Raif's stomach clenched in absolute fury. He turned back

to Roxanne, controlling the urge to go after his uncle and demand answers. "Is that one of the men who kidnapped you?"

Roxanne nodded mutely. Her voice was a raspy whisper. "He was in the basement when I arrived. They were blackmailing my sister Kendra. They told her they would kill me if she didn't give them information."

Raif's pulse was escalating from anger to fury.

It was his uncle? His own uncle had been mixed up in this mess all along? He didn't understand how the pieces fit together, but he knew he would get answers. He would not rest until he got answers.

Blackmailing Roxanne's sister Kendra had to be at the core of the plan to hurt Ann and Waverly's.

He extracted his cell phone and handed it to Roxanne. "Call your sister. Tell her you're safe. Tell her we're bringing you home."

When Ann walked into the office after a lengthy meeting with the board, Kendra was bent over her desk, talking on the telephone. Tears were streaming down her face. She wiped her nose, blowing noisily into a tissue.

"Yes," she said shakily into the receiver. "I understand. I'll be there. I love you so much, Roxy. Goodbye."

It was bad news. It had to be bad news about her sister. Whatever the details, Ann's heart went out to Kendra. She felt her own eyes tear up in sympathy.

Kendra's hand shook as she replaced the receiver, and she sobbed a fresh round of tears.

"Kendra?" Ann said, obviously startling her.

Kendra swiveled in her chair.

Ann quickly approached. "Is it Roxanne? Is she worse?"

Kendra gave a bit of a hysterical laugh, covering her mouth with her hand, the tears continuing to stream down her face.

Ann's only thought was that Roxanne must be fatally ill. She crouched down, putting her hand on Kendra's arm.

"What can I do? How can I help?"

Kendra shook her head. "It's okay. It's good news. She's been freed."

"She's not sick anymore?"

Kendra shook her head more vigorously. "She was never sick. I'm so sorry, Ann. I lied to you." Kendra's face crumpled. "I lied to all of you."

"You lied about your sister?" Ann was growing confused. What would be the point of lying? It wasn't as though Kendra had asked for money or anything.

"She was kidnapped," said Kendra, bitterness strengthening her voice. "Months ago. They kidnapped her, and Dalton Rothschild has been blackmailing me ever since."

Ann's blood ran completely cold. She could barely force out the question. "Blackmailing you for what?"

"Information. On Waverly's. And especially on the *Gold Heart* statue."

"You've been spying on us?" Ann was forced to steady herself on the back of Kendra's chair. All this time, with everything Waverley's and Ann herself had been going through, Kendra had been operating against them?

Kendra's expression crumpled. "They were going to kill her."

Ann could see Kendra's genuine fear. And after what she and Kalila had been through, she knew Roxanne had been in true danger.

"Where is she?" Ann asked in worry. "Is she safe?"

"She's in Rayas."

For a second, Ann thought she might faint. She slumped down, sitting full on the floor, her mind galloping.

The night at the docks. It all flooded back to her. She'd thought she was hallucinating. She wasn't. But she hadn't seen Kendra. She'd seen Roxanne.

She should have done something. She should have asked questions right then and there.

Kendra interrupted her thoughts. "Someone named Tariq is bringing her home on a private jet."

Ann shook herself back to the present. This was no time for self-recrimination. Tariq was coming to New York. Did he have some answers? Did Dalton know he was caught? Would he try to run? Or would he hurt someone in a last-ditch attempt to cover things up?

Ann fumbled for her phone.

She scanned her call history until she found Heidi Shaw's number. She pressed the call button and let it ring.

While she waited, she reached up to squeeze Kendra's hand. "Tariq will take good care of Roxanne."

Kendra swallowed.

"Agent Shaw," came the greeting.

"Heidi? It's Ann Richardson. I think I need your help. Do you still want to make an arrest in our big, international case?"

Eleven

Prince Mallik's interrogation went quickly. The old man's hostility was no match for Jordan's training.

It turned out Dalton had heard back-channel rumors of Roark's *Gold Heart* discovery. Taking advantage of the information, he'd concocted the plot to hurt Ann and sink Waverly's in one fell swoop. Before Roark had time to announce his find, Dalton had contacted Prince Mallik, playing on the old man's greed and bitterness, convincing him the statue's theft would discredit Raif and bring bad luck to the Khouri family.

Once Mallik had implicated Roark, Ann and Waverly's were caught up in the growing scandal. Kendra's information had ensured Dalton made all the right moves to sink Waverly's. While in Rayas, the ensuing scandal and chaos provided an opening for Mallik to take power when King Safwah died.

After the interrogation, Raif took steps to keep his uncle's involvement under wraps, and Prince Mallik was quickly banished to a remote estate in the north of Rayas, to be held under guard for the rest of his life. A large sum was settled on Roxanne and Kendra in restitution.

Stateside, Agent Heidi Shaw had been pivotal in the arrest and interrogation of Dalton. The *Gold Heart* statue was recovered from one of the secret tunnels in Valhan Palace. Mallik had hidden it there from the beginning, moving it when Ann arrived at the palace, and setting off the internal alarm.

The *Gold Heart* now sat in its glass dome in the great foyer of Valhan Palace, in place for Raif's coronation. Wearing the robes and jewels of his ancestors, he wound his way past the statue and into the grand hall.

There, statesmen and dignitaries from all around the world looked on. Family, friends and well-wishers bowed their heads as he passed. He was about to step into the role he'd been trained for from birth. But through it all, his thoughts strayed to Ann.

He wanted her here by his side. He wanted her comfort and her counsel. He wanted to fight with her, joke with her and make love with her.

But instead of the love of his life, he had Tariq's list of fifty perfectly acceptable young Rayasian women back on his desk. He needed to consider them. But he couldn't even bring himself to read it.

His one consolation was that Kalila was happy. She would now need to take a larger role in the country's governance. To his credit, Niles understood her duty and was ready to support her.

For the coronation, Kalila sat at the far end of the hall, on the smaller of two thrones. She was next to the chancellor who would preside over the ancient ceremony.

Raif had Tariq at the head of his honor guard. And he also had Niles in the ceremony. Soon to be the newest member of the royal family, Niles was already proving himself an adroit diplomat. At least Kalila had good taste in her choice of husband.

Perhaps she could help Raif choose a wife.

The minute the thought formed, Raif's entire body rebelled. As he came to a stop in front of the chancellor, he couldn't help glancing at Jacx, who had finally agreed to become an admiral. He remembered the fateful day when Jacx had stepped up to marry Princess Salima.

A crazy thought formed in Raif's head. What would happen if he pulled a "Daud" and backed out of the coronation ceremony? He could do as Daud had done, tell the chancellor that he was sorry, but he loved another, and he couldn't be king.

How would Kalila and Niles feel about reigning in his stead?

He looked to his cousin.

Her smile was serene. She was absolutely in love with Niles, and the two were going to be very happy together. Raif couldn't do anything to disrupt that. And he couldn't disrupt Rayas. His people had been through enough.

The chancellor began the ceremony, and Raif stood at rapt attention.

Though the Rayasian coronation hadn't been covered by any of the major Western news channels, Ann was able to find a video of it posted to the internet the next day. She maximized the screen, squinting to watch Raif in the distance. The video was eighteen hours old, but it was surreal seeing him walk the length of the grand hall, taking his vows, sitting on his throne, the crown being held over his head.

A knock sounded on her apartment door.

Ann froze the screen, padding across the carpet in her bare feet. It was Saturday morning. She was still dressed in her Rangers T-shirt and plaid boxer shorts. She hadn't showered and was seriously considering the pint of Häagen-Dazs buried in her apartment freezer.

As Ann had guessed, it was Darby at her door.

"Did you find it?" Darby asked. She was freshly showered, dressed in blue jeans, a pink tank top and a pair of sneakers. Her damp hair was pulled back in a perky ponytail.

"I did," said Ann. "It's not very good, but he's there." She clicked the mouse, bringing the video back to life, sitting down while Darby stood behind her.

The ceremony was in Rayasian. So, when the chancellor suddenly stepped back from Raif and lowered the crown, Ann couldn't figure out what was going on.

Kalila's head turned suddenly, and she stared at Raif. At the same time, the men of the honor guard began speaking to one another. Someone stepped between Raif and the chancellor who was still holding the crown in his hands.

"What the heck?" Darby muttered.

"I think that's Tariq," said Ann, squinting at the frustratingly small image.

"Do you think maybe he's sick? Like a heart attack?"

"He's a pretty healthy guy," Ann responded. "And nobody seems to be panicking. It's like they've suddenly decided to hold a meeting."

The video stopped. Ann clicked her mouse, hoping to get more, but the play bar zipped to the end and stopped.

"Well, that's bizarre," said Darby.

Bizarre didn't begin to cover it. Ann wanted to shout at the screen in frustration.

"Do another search," Darby advised. "Maybe there's another video."

Ann returned to the search engine, typing in *Rayas* and *coronation*.

The hits that came up were mostly articles rather than videos. "Coronation Interrupted," "Valhan Palace Issues Statement," and "Speculation of Abdication."

Ann and Darby gaped at the screen.

"Abdication?" Darby asked in awe.

"You know what the tabloids are like," Ann felt compelled to put in, even though her stomach was beginning to churn.

There was no way in the world that Raif would do anything detrimental to Rayas. He loved his country far too dearly to harm it. But something was definitely wrong. She clicked on the "Valhan Palace Issues Statement" article, hoping to get the official story.

The intercom buzzed.

"You get it," she said to Darby, watching while the article started to load.

Darby headed for the speaker. "Hello?"

"Ann?" asked a deep, accented male voice.

Ann's heart contracted. She whirled around.

"Ann?" Raif's voice came again.

"Is it him?" Darby hissed.

Ann nodded helplessly.

"Come in," said Darby.

"Don't," Ann shouted.

But it was too late, Darby had already pressed the front door's unlock button.

"Why did you do that?" Ann demanded, coming to her feet.

"Do you want to get changed?" asked Darby, scanning Ann's outfit. "Quick, go wash your face and put something else on. I'll stall him."

"No, I don't want to change." Ann didn't want to impress Raif. She wanted to learn how to live without Raif. And she couldn't do that if he was standing in her apartment.

"At least you can get the straight scoop," Darby reasoned, hand on the front door handle as she waited for Raif's knock.

"Why would he come here?" Ann struggled to stay calm. "Do you think anybody would have seen him?" Ann craned her neck, gazing out the window, praying there were no reporters on the street.

"It might be the obvious," said Darby.

"What obvious?"

Darby gave her a look that questioned her intellect. "He came here to tell you he gave up his kingdom."

Everything inside Ann went still. "That's not the obvious. That's ridiculous."

Never mind that she'd played with the idea more than once

while she was in Rayas. But it was a crazy fantasy, and Raif was an incredibly stable man.

He only managed one knock before Darby swung open the door.

The sight of Darby seemed to take him aback. "I'm looking for Ann Richardson."

Darby turned to look at Ann, and Raif followed her gaze.

He smiled then, and Ann thought her insides might melt. A million questions surged in her mind, and a rush of hormones roared through her system. She had made absolutely no progress whatsoever in getting over him.

"What happened?" she blurted out.

He looked to Darby. "Do you mind?"

"I'm outta here," Darby quickly put in, moving through the doorway. She turned and grinned. "Much as I'm dying, absolutely dying to find out what's going on. You better call me," she ordered Ann.

"I'll call," Ann promised, her gaze never leaving Raif. He was the sexiest man alive. Despite everything, she was incredibly glad to see him. But he had no business whatsoever showing up here.

The door closed behind Darby.

"What happened?" Ann repeated. "I saw something on the internet, you, the chancellor, the Grand Hall. But then everything stopped."

He took a few paces toward her. "I'm happy to see you, too, Ann."

"I am *not* happy to see you." They'd been through all this. They'd made the tough choice. They'd said their goodbyes. "Why are you here? Your people need you, Raif."

"My people can wait."

"For what?"

He moved closer. "I stopped the coronation."

Her stomach clenched. She didn't want to ask why. She didn't want to know why. This could only end badly for everyone. She swallowed. "Why?"

"Because I can't do it without you, Ann."

"*No*." Her knees went weak.

Raif quickly grasped her arms to steady her. "I gave the chancellor an offer he couldn't refuse. And I wasn't bluffing."

"No," she repeated, voice gravelly, shaking her head in denial. "You can't, Raif. You can't."

Rayas was everything to him.

"Marry me, Ann."

This wasn't real. This couldn't be happening. She had to be asleep in her bed. Maybe it was still last night. Maybe she hadn't woken up yet, hadn't found the video.

She waited, but nothing happened.

She pinched herself, but nothing happened.

She searched her mind for an argument to sway him, some words that would help him put things in perspective. She grasped at an idea. "Do you want to sleep with me again? Is that it? Because we could—"

He frowned. "This isn't about sleeping with you, Ann."

"The sex was really good," she rattled on. "Don't you think it was good? It's probably just the sex."

"I want to *marry* you."

"That's not possible." A fling was one thing. They could come back from a fling. But, once he came to his senses, which he most certainly would, there was no way to undo a marriage. Not in Rayas. Kalila had been clear about that.

"Why not?" he asked in a perfectly reasonable tone.

She struggled not to yell at him for being so obtuse. "Because you're a crown prince. You're about to be a king." She gestured helplessly at her computer monitor. "You know, just as soon as they finish the YouTube video."

"The chancellor has agreed," said Raif.

She gave her head a wild shake. "No. I can't. I live here in New York. You live over there. I have a life. You have... I mean, wow, *do you ever have a life*."

"I know it's a lot to take on."

"No, you don't. You can't even imagine. You've never been

normal, Raif. And you don't want me. Not really. Deep down inside, you want the young Rayasian virgin with the brown eyes and the dark hair."

"I don't," he told her with conviction.

"You do."

"I'm letting Kalila marry Niles."

That got Ann's attention. "Really?"

"Really."

She found herself cracking an involuntary smile. "That's wonderful. She's an amazing woman, Raif."

"I know she's an amazing woman. But I only told you that to prove you don't have to be Rayasian to marry into our royal family. Kalila's setting the precedent."

"It's not the same thing."

"It's exactly the same thing." Raif clenched his jaw then sighed. "Fine. Don't answer me now. Take some time to think about it. But know that you're messing with everything I dreamed about all the way across the Atlantic."

"I'm not going to change my mind," she warned him. She wouldn't. She couldn't. They were playing with some really serious stuff here, and one of them had to keep their head out of the clouds.

Raif's expression relaxed and he leaned slowly forward to kiss her hairline. "I'll give you some time and space to take it all in. I'll go away for a few hours."

"A few hours?"

"Think about it, Ann."

Even though she had no intention of changing her mind, a few hours didn't seem like much time to contemplate your entire life.

"I'll come back," he finished.

"Be careful. Don't talk to reporters."

Raif grinned. "I'll be fine. Jordan will take good care of me."

"Jordan's here?"

"Yes. So is Tariq."

"Really?" She reflexively glanced around Raif, wondering if Tariq was lurking in the hall.

"Hey, don't act like you're more interested in seeing Tariq than me."

"I like Tariq."

"You love me."

"Raif, this is crazy. And I mean that literally."

"It's not crazy. And I'm not crazy. And you need to think about this." He kissed her mouth this time, gently, fleetingly. "I'm going to leave you alone. Don't you dare try to run away."

"I wouldn't—" Okay, maybe she might.

"I have men watching the street."

"You do not."

"I do. They won't let me travel with less than a hundred people. I honestly don't know what to do with them all."

"This isn't a joke, Raif."

"No. It isn't a joke. I understand it's a big decision."

"I can't be what you want me to be."

He smiled at her then, and her heart tripped all over itself. "I want you to be you."

He took a step back, then another, and another, until he let himself out of her apartment.

"No, you don't," she whispered to the closed door.

He didn't want her to be Ann Richardson. He wanted her to be the queen of Rayas. She didn't have the first idea of how to be a queen. She didn't know Rayasian customs or protocol. She couldn't even speak the language.

For a moment, she did think about running away. Running away and hiding until Raif got over this ridiculous notion. But that would be a cop-out, and it would just postpone the inevitable. She had to be tough and stand her ground. She'd pretend to think about it for a few hours. Then she'd tell him no, send him away from her, fully and finally.

The thought made her cold, and she started to shake. She curled up on the couch, wrapping her arms around herself.

A short time later, Darby knocked on the door, and it was all Ann could do to walk over and fling it open.

To her astonishment, it wasn't Darby standing in the hall. It was an older man, a man she vaguely recognized. She'd seen him in photographs, but she'd never met him in person.

"Rutherford Waverly?" she asked, uncertainty combining with the trembling in her voice.

"Ann." He smiled in a way that made her feel as if they were old friends.

She glanced both ways down her hall. "I don't understand."

What was he doing here? Though once the chairman of the Waverly's board, Rutherford had been a silent, shadowy figure as long as Ann had been employed by the company. She certainly never expected him to know where she lived, never mind show up at her doorstep.

"Do you have a minute?" he asked, his tone polite, quite formal. "There's something we need to discuss."

She couldn't help but wonder if he knew about Raif. He must be aware of the *Gold Heart* scandal. Did he know she'd gone to Rayas? Did he think they were having an affair?

She shook herself back to life. "Of course, Mr. Waverly."

"Rutherford, please." He stepped into her apartment, taking it all in.

She wished she'd taken the time to vacuum and dust since coming home. Then she suddenly remembered she was still in her pajamas.

"Please, sit down," she offered, moving a couple of magazines off the couch. "I'm sorry about the mess. Let me go change."

"No need." He waved her off. "Unexpected company needs to take what they get. I am sorry to intrude. But what I have to say can't wait."

He stood poised, expectant, obviously waiting for her to sit down. So, she perched on the edge of an armchair.

He sat down on the couch. "I'm afraid I bring unsettling news."

Ann actually fought the urge to smile. Rutherford had no idea the act he was following. There was nothing in the world that could top Raif's visit for unsettling.

"Waverly's is holding an emergency board meeting as we speak."

Okay, that was a pretty close second. For the board to convene on December 22nd, the issue had to be significant. Ann normally participated in board meetings, and she hadn't heard anything about this one.

"Is it because of Kendra?" she asked.

Ann hadn't fired her assistant, and she'd offered to testify on Kendra's behalf if the police decided to press charges. It was true that Kendra had stolen secrets from Waverly's. But she'd only done it because she had feared for her sister's life. Ann didn't honestly know what she would do if one of her own family members were threatened.

"They're voting on firing you," said Rutherford.

Ann swallowed, realizing she'd become too cavalier about her job security. "Any specific reason?"

"On balance, your fitness as a leader."

Ann stood. "I see." She crossed restlessly to the window. "Do you happen to know who will win?"

"As much as I can tell, you'll lose by one vote."

Ann wrapped her mind around that. She'd feared it might happen for several months now. But her fear had been greatly diminished when Raif had confirmed the authenticity of Roark's *Gold Heart*. It had diminished again when Dalton had been arrested.

"Unless," said Rutherford.

Ann turned.

There was a glint in his eyes and an impish smile on his aging face.

"Unless?" she prompted.

"Unless you might be interested in moseying on down to the board meeting."

"To plead my case?" Ann wasn't sure what she could possibly say that would change anyone's mind. Everyone knew the facts.

Rutherford shook his head. "To watch me exercise my ex-officio right to vote."

It took her a moment to understand. "You'd vote in my favor?"

"Absolutely."

Ann was confused.

"What's in it for you?" she dared to ask, uncomfortable with not understanding the entire situation.

"I like you," he said simply. "I like Edwina and the others that support you. And I'm not at all fond of those who are working against you. Waverly's is stronger with you at the helm, Ann Richardson. You've worked hard. You've accomplished a lot for the shareholders. Your reward for that shouldn't be to have the board show you the door."

Emotions that were simmering close to the surface threatened to spill over. Ann's throat closed in.

"Thank you" was all she could manage.

Rutherford came to his feet. "So, do you want to humor an old man and have some fun?"

"Yes. I do."

"For that, you might want to change your clothes."

Watching Rutherford at the board meeting had been a treat for Ann. From the second he'd walked in, to the moment he informed the members he was planning to vote in Ann's favor, he'd had their undivided attention. Some members, like Edwina, were clearly thrilled to see him back. Others were clearly angry at his interference. But he'd pulled it off with aplomb.

Astonishingly, Ann was able to push Raif from her mind for a short time. But after the vote, during the drive home, and especially after Rutherford had dropped her off in front of the building, Raif was taking up her every thought.

Darby had obviously been waiting, because the minute Ann

walked by her door, she rushed out, falling into step in the hallway.

"What happened?" she demanded. "Where did you go?"

"Waverly's," Ann answered, reaching into her purse for her keys. It took her a moment to find them, and she resisted the urge to curse. She had no patience for this.

"What about Raif?" Darby asked.

"Raif left."

"Why?"

Ann twisted the key in the dead bolt. "He wanted to give me some time."

"Some time to go to Waverly's?"

Ann pushed open the door. She wanted to talk, but she didn't want to talk. She wished Darby would leave. Then again, she was incredibly glad Darby was here.

"Ann?" Darby prompted.

"Some time to decide whether or not to marry him."

Darby stopped dead in her tracks.

Ann closed the door.

"Yeah." She agreed with Darby's shocked reaction. "That's pretty much what I said, too."

"But, that's wonderful," Darby sputtered.

"Wonderful? *Wonderful?* How is it wonderful?"

"He loves you."

"I already knew that."

"And he wants you to be his wife, to be his…" Darby clamped her mouth closed.

"You can say it," Ann drawled. But then she halted, focusing on an unfamiliar package sitting on her coffee table. "What's that?"

Darby moved up beside her. "It looks like a present."

The flat, rectangular package was wrapped in gold paper, with shiny purple ribbon and a sparkling bow.

"Where did it come from?" Ann looked suspiciously at Darby.

"Not from me," she affirmed. "I only knocked on your door while you were gone. I didn't come inside."

Ann dropped her purse and circled the table. She didn't like this. Dalton might be locked up, but with all the strangeness in her life lately, she didn't trust the package for one second.

"Do you think it might explode?" she asked out loud.

"It's a present, not a bomb."

"If you were sending someone a bomb, wouldn't you wrap it as a present?"

"I don't think it's big enough to be a bomb."

Ann frowned at her friend. "Based on your many years of explosive and demolitions training?"

"Based on watching many movies of the week." Darby leaned down. "It's not ticking."

"Don't touch it," Ann warned.

"Oh, good grief." Darby picked up the package and shook it. Ann reflexively jumped back.

"It barely weighs a thing," said Darby.

"I'm sure there are such things as microbombs."

"That's ridiculous." Darby pulled on the ribbon. It came untied, and the bow fell off with it.

"This is a bad idea," said Ann.

"Maybe it was him," Darby returned, sliding her fingernail under the tape.

"Raif? No. I was sitting in here with Rutherford after Raif left. It couldn't have been him."

"Who's Rutherford?"

"Someone from Waverly's. Hey, I get to keep my job."

"That's great." Darby removed the paper, revealing a plain white cardboard box.

"That's where I went. To a board meeting. Rutherford made them keep me."

"Good for Rutherford. Do you think this is from Rutherford?"

"Maybe," Ann allowed slowly. He could have put it there while she was changing her clothes. Maybe it was a congratulations gift. Rutherford had known when they left the apartment that he was likely to succeed in helping her keep her job.

Darby handed over the box, and Ann accepted it. Reassured that it wasn't about to explode in her hands, Ann sat down. She lifted the lid, revealing a beautiful white silk fabric. Translucent, it was trimmed with an intricate purple scroll pattern, laced with fine gold thread.

Lifting it from the box, Ann recognized it as a Rayasian head scarf.

"How on earth..." she mused in wonder.

It was the most delicate scarf she had ever seen, and she was fairly certain the jewels sewn into the trim were real.

"It's Rayasian," she explained to Darby. "All the women wear them on their heads. They're beautiful."

"Show me," Darby encouraged.

"Why would Rutherford leave a Rayasian scarf?"

"I've been listening all morning," said Darby. "Nobody else was here. Put it on."

Ann was tempted. Kalila had demonstrated how to wear them a few times, and Ann was willing to give it a try.

"I'll be right back," she told Darby, taking the box and the scarf and moving down the hallway to a mirror.

It took her a few tries, but she got it comfortable halfway back on her head, looped loosely around her neck. The colors suited her, and she smiled.

Then, when she lifted the empty box, she found an envelope in the bottom. Stomach fluttering in anticipation of an answer, she opened the flap. Inside was a note, written in a scrawling masculine hand, on crisp white paper.

Ann, remember your first day at Hampton Heights private school? How strange the uniform felt? You learned then, and you know now, you will fit in. You'll love your new life.

There was no signature. She flipped the paper over and then

checked the envelope, but there was no proof that Rutherford had written the note. Everyone at Waverly's knew she'd gone to Hampton Heights. But how could he have known how she felt those first days and weeks? And he couldn't possibly have guessed how she felt about Raif.

"Ann?" Darby called from the living room, and Ann turned to go back.

Ten steps later, she came face-to-face with Raif.

It was hard to know who'd had the bigger shock.

The smile on his face disappeared, and his complexion paled. "Where did you get that?"

Ann's fingers automatically rose to the scarf. "I don't know," she confessed.

He moved closer, his jaw tight. "Where, Ann?"

"Raif, what's wrong?"

Darby sidled sideways toward the door. "I'll, uh, just step…" She opened the door and left.

"It can't be?" Raif rasped, still staring at the scarf in obvious shock.

"I don't know where it came from. It was in a box."

She didn't want to upset him. She wanted to marry him. Whoever had written the note was right. Ann loved Raif, and she was willing to turn her life upside down to be with him.

She could adapt to Rayas. She could learn to be queen. Raif would be there to help her, and so would Kalila. Surely, someone could teach her Rayasian.

His expression didn't change.

"Have you changed your mind?" she asked on a pained whisper.

His tone turned raw. "I have not changed my mind. My mind is more made up than ever." He reached out to touch the scarf. "This was my grandmother's."

"Is it a fake?" It had to be a fake.

Raif shook his head. "It's the real thing. You're the real thing."

She wordlessly handed Raif the note.

His eyes stayed locked with hers for a very long time. Then, ever so slowly, he looked at the paper.

When his gaze came back to her it was soft, his voice softer. "They are right. And I thank them. You are my queen."

In that moment, tension, fear and worry evaporated from Ann's body. She inclined her head. "Your Majesty. I will be honored to marry you."

He put a finger to her chin, raising it up. "The queen does not bow. My darling, I will shower you in silks and jewels and love."

She tilted her head to meet his kiss. "I only need the love."

"You will have it," he breathed. "Every day of your life."

Twelve

Since Raif had always found it expedient to give people offers they couldn't refuse, he guaranteed Waverly's a hefty percentage above their estimate on the *Gold Heart* if they were quite willing to go to auction before New Year's. So, December 31st they were hosting the sale.

They ended up with a dozen bidders for the late afternoon auction, and Raif was forced to pay more than he'd planned. It hadn't mattered. The *Gold Heart* wasn't going anywhere except home to Rayas. The cost had been irrelevant.

The auction over, everybody seemed to be in the mood to party. The bidders and Waverly's staff and guests were invited into the auction house's largest room for an informal dinner. In honor of New Year's, the walls and ceiling were decorated with balloons, streamers and stylized clocks. The tables were covered in white linen, the china and stemware was blue, and each table had a candle at the center, surrounded by a crystal bowl of blue and silver balls.

A string quartet played on a raised dais at one end of the room as people made their way to tables.

A distinguished-looking older man approached Raif.

"Congratulations," the man offered, holding out his hand for a surprisingly hearty shake. "Rutherford Waverly."

"Raif Khouri," Raif offered.

"I know," Rutherford responded with a smile.

Raif's gaze rested on Ann, who was on the opposite side of the room, working like a pro as she chatted with the various employees and guests. She wore a black dress, formfitting and full-length. The sweetheart neckline was made demure by his grandmother's scarf looped around her neck.

Since Rutherford had been the only other guest in Ann's apartment that day, and since Raif had discovered the man had a penchant for meddling—in a positive way—Raif guessed he had to be the one who gave Ann the scarf.

"How did you get it?" Raif asked Rutherford.

The man didn't pretend to misunderstand. "I've lived a long life," he said simply. "You don't do that without developing a few contacts."

"In Rayas?" Raif asked, letting his skepticism show through.

"A friend of a friend," Rutherford responded with a secretive smile.

"I heard another story about the Tarlington diamond ring. It seems it was also left with a mysterious note, and it benefited another Waverly-associated couple, Carter McCay and Macy Tarlington. That sealed Carter's marriage proposal."

"Interesting." Rutherford's expression remained inscrutable.

"A long-lost letter from Roark Black's mother, telling him he was a Waverly? An angel statue that had been lost to Avery Cullen," Raif probed further.

Rutherford wasn't the only one with investigative capacity. Raif had discovered that many of the couples associated with Waverly's had been the beneficiaries of mysterious happenings that helped their romances. Raif was convinced Rutherford was Waverly's very own romantic benefactor. He admired the old man for both his caring and his ingenuity.

"Not everyone can rely on good-luck statues," said Rutherford."

"I owe you my thanks," said Raif. "Somehow you knew exactly what to tell her."

"I've watched Ann for many years," Rutherford responded. "She's a good girl. She deserves to be happy."

"I take it you think I can make her happy." Raif had wondered many times if taking her away from New York was the best thing for her.

"You've already made her happy," said Rutherford.

A waiter passed by, and Rutherford deftly lifted two glasses of champagne from the man's silver tray, handing one to Raif.

"Are you going to tell them?" asked Raif, thinking Rutherford deserved credit for his hard work and ingenuity in helping so many couples.

Rutherford gave him a wink. "Watch this."

He strode across the room to step up to the quartet's raised dais.

The move had clearly been prearranged. A musician immediately handed Rutherford a microphone, and then the quartet played a loud flourish, gaining everyone's attention.

"Good evening," Rutherford said into the mike.

There was a round of polite applause for the former chairman of the board.

"Thank you." He gave a head bob. "And thank you all for coming out tonight, especially our bidders, and particularly Raif Khouri, our successful bidder. I know I speak for everyone at Waverly's when I congratulate you on repatriating your statue to Rayas."

The crowd turned Raif's way, offering up another round of applause.

Raif caught Ann's gaze, and her smile seemed to warm his entire body. He couldn't wait to get her back to his hotel suite. No, that wasn't quite right. He couldn't wait to get her back to Rayas. He was impatient to introduce her to his people.

"I know many of you haven't seen me lately," Rutherford

continued. "But I've been close by. I've been paying attention. I've learned a few things along the way. And, I have to say, I am proud of each and every one of you."

The crowd was quiet, obviously curious.

"Vance and Charlotte," said Rutherford to Vance Waverly and his former secretary and true love, "I was so pleased to see you work your way through the mystery that was keeping you apart." He looked to wealthy ranch owner Carter McCay, his arm around Macy, who wore her gorgeous heirloom diamond on her ring finger. "Carter, I'm envious. You have an amazing woman there in Macy. Treasure her." He moved on to art-expert Marcus Price and the glowingly pregnant Avery. "Marcus and Avery, I know you already know this, but you are blessed. Your own statue is more meaningful to you than all the jewels in the world."

Raif could see the moment some of the crowd clued in. Ann was one of the first whose eyes went wide. Few people knew about Marcus and Avery's angel statue, and those who did immediately realized that Rutherford had to have been behind it.

Rutherford looked to billionaire Chase Harrington and Vanessa Partridge, the woman who had changed his life. "Chase and Vanessa, your hearts are filled with love for your children. Together, you're building them a heritage. I'm thrilled to have even the smallest part in that."

Vanessa whispered something to Chase, and the man seemed to look at Rutherford in a whole new light.

Ann moved along the edges of the room toward Raif. He immediately headed to meet her.

"Roark, you deserve to know your roots, and you deserve your lovely and wonderful wife, Elizabeth. I'm sure you all realize what I'm saying. I love you all dearly, including you, Ann. And I am so very pleased to help launch you into your new life. Whatever you need, Ann. Please know I'm here."

Rutherford paused for a second and cleared his throat.

Ann slipped into Raif's arms.

"Did you know he'd done all of it?" she whispered to Raif.

"I guessed," said Raif. "Okay, I also sleuthed. What's the point of having an intelligence service if you're not going to use it?"

Raif had learned that Rutherford had suffered a broken heart after falling in love with the daughter of a chief business rival. Though he'd been pulled from the day-to-day running of the company, he continued to care deeply about the company, and to care deeply about those involved in it. He was a true romantic, not wanting anyone else to suffer heartache.

Ann's smile was dazzling.

Rutherford raised his champagne glass. "To all of you. My friends, my family, my colleagues. I'll be resuming a more active role in Waverly's, with Vance and Charles's long-lost son Roark by my side. I'll miss Ann as she starts her new life as a queen. But I look forward to working with you all."

The hear, hears were followed by enthusiastic applause.

"He's an incredible man," Ann said to Raif.

"You are an incredible woman," Raif returned, pride tightening his chest. "Your beauty aside, you have skills and talent. Have I mentioned that Rayas has a national artifacts collection? It's the largest in the region."

Her eyes lit up. "Really? Do you think I could work with them?"

"You'll be the queen. You can do whatever you want."

She sighed and leaned into him, voice going breathy. "I love you, Your Majesty."

"Come home with me," he whispered. "Come home with me right now."

"To the hotel?"

"To Rayas. We'll fly tonight." He kissed her temple, lowering his voice. "We'll make love amongst the stars, and ring in the New Year halfway between your world and mine."

"Oh, yes," she agreed with a satisfied smile.

Raif put a hand on the small of her back, gently guiding her toward the exit. Most of the attention was still on Rutherford, but a few people wished Ann and Raif good-night as they passed.

She was happy to leave this way. She'd be back soon—and probably often—and she'd have time to touch base with her colleagues. But, for now, she had a wedding to plan and a brand-new life to start.

She rested her head on Raif's shoulder, and his hand tightened on her waist.

"My love," he whispered.

"My life," she returned in a breath, heart filling with anticipation and desire.

* * * * *